zorgamazoo

robert paul weston

razOr bill

Zorgamazoo

RAZORBILL

Published by the Penguin Group
Penguin Young Readers Group
345 Hudson Street, New York, New York 10014, U.S.A.
Penguin Group (USA) Inc., 375 Hudson Street, New York, New York 10014, U.S.A.
Penguin Group (Canada), 90 Eglinton Avenue East, Suite 700, Toronto, Ontario, Canada M4P 2Y3 (a division of Pearson Penguin Canada Inc.)
Penguin Books Ltd, 80 Strand, London WC2R 0RL, England
Penguin Ireland, 25 St Stephen's Green, Dublin 2, Ireland (a division of Penguin Books Ltd)
Penguin Group (Australia), 250 Camberwell Road, Camberwell, Victoria 3124, Australia (a division of Pearson Australia Group Pty Ltd)
Penguin Books India Pvt Ltd, 11 Community Centre, Panchsheel Park, New Delhi – 110 017, India
Penguin Group (NZ), 67 Apollo Drive, Rosedale, North Shore 0632, New Zealand
(a division of Pearson New Zealand Ltd.)

Penguin Books (South Africa) (Pty) Ltd, 24 Sturdee Avenue, Rosebank, Johannesburg 2196, South Africa

Penguin Books Ltd, Registered Offices: 80 Strand, London WC2R 0RL, England

20 19 18 17 16 15 14 13 12 11

Library of Congress Cataloging-in-Publication Data is available

Razorbill hardcover ISBN: 978-1-59514-199-6
Razorbill paperback ISBN: 978-1-59514-295-5

Printed in the United States of America
Book Design by Christian Fuenfhausen
Illustrations by Víctor Rivas Villa

Praise for Zorgamazoo

2009 E.B. WHITE READ ALOUD HONOR

2010 SILVER BIRCH AWARD WINNER
The Silver Birch Award® is given by Canadian children in grades 3-6 to their favorite book of the year.

2010 CALIFORNIA YOUNG READER MEDAL NOMINEE

2011 PACIFIC NORTHWEST LIBRARY ASSOCIATION YOUNG READERS CHOICE AWARD NOMINEE

★"A natural descendant of the works of Dr. Seuss and Roald Dahl while hewing close to the droll atmospherics of Edward Gorey and Lemony Snicket.

—*Booklist* (Starred; Top Ten Debut)

"Just begging to be read aloud! —*DPL Kid's Blog*

"One of the most exciting children's books to hit the shelves in a long time . . ." —*Canadian Children's Book News*

"If Seuss and Dahl collaborated early in their careers, something similar might have resulted. . . . Snicket fans and reluctant readers not afraid of a peek at verse will likely feel right at home." —*Kirkus*

"Give this one to readers who enjoy a little nonsense."

—*School Library Journal*

"There's something infectious, contagious, sublime/about a 280-plus-page novel written completely in rhyme. . . ."

—*The Globe and Mail*

"If you can imagine the spawn of the Harry Potter series and Dr. Seuss's "There's a Wocket in My Pocket," you are on the right track to understanding the magical, hilarious whiz-bang creativity of *Zorgamazoo*."

—Tegan, Queen Anne Books (Seattle)

"A story rich in clever wordplay, unusual characters, and fantastic circumstances . . . The book's illustrations are reminiscent of the oval-eyed, twiggish vulnerability of Tim Burton's creations, and the details of the story traverse some of the same dark territory."

—*Quill & Quire*

"Two hundred and eighty-three pages of flawless rhyme whisk us through joy, sorrow, suspense, giggles, bliss, shock and triumph in this beautifully illustrated and designed adventure in friendship, self-discovery and the power of engagement."

—Just One More Book

"A well-constructed story with fully realized characters and plenty of humor. The rhyme is almost flawless. . . . Fancifully frightening illustrations and typographical trickery create an inviting visual package."

—*The Horn Book Magazine*

CHAPTER 1
a shadowy form

Here is a story

that's stranger than strange.

Before we begin you may want to arrange:

a blanket,
a cushion,
a comfortable seat,
and maybe some cocoa and something to eat.

I'll warn you, of course, before we commence,
my story is eerie and full of suspense,
brimming with danger and narrow escapes,
and creatures of many remarkable shapes.
Dragons and ogres and gorgons and more,
and creatures you've not even heard of before.
And faraway places? There's plenty of those!
(And menacing villains to tingle your toes.)

So ready your mettle and steady your heart.
It's time for my story's mysterious start…

We begin in a subway, under the ground,
where people in trains go rolling around,
in hurrying haste and in scurrying mobs,
wandering off to their ponderous jobs.

Much of the time they would linger in vain.
They would stand in the station awaiting a train.
They would push in between the ticket machines,
like fish huddled into a tin of sardines.

They clutched at the purses and cases they brought,
anxious and angry and overly wrought,

hoping a train would come barreling past,
pick them up quick, and dash away fast!

There was one little girl who waited as well:
a girl by the name of

Katrina Katrell.

While everyone else was busy or bored,
this one little girl should not be ignored.
For unlike the crowd, she was never inert.
Her senses were sharp and awake and alert.

She kept to herself, but she wasn't alone.
She was joined by her guardian, Mrs. Krabone,
who stood with Katrina, clutching her hand,
in the flickering light of the passenger stand.

They were hunched near the tunnel
    of mortar and brick
where the lighting was dim and shadows were thick,
where Katrina was curious, squinting her eye…
she could swear that a *creature* was shuffling by.

At first it was vague, just a shadowy form,
like a ship in a mist or the fog of a storm.
So she gaped with a steady, unfaltering stare,
to determine for certain:

Was anything there?

Yet try as she might, the tunnel was black,
obscuring the path of the train and the track.

She nearly was ready to give up her search,
when the subway arrived in a lumbering lurch.
It showered the station in glimmering light,
and that's when she saw something scurry from sight!

"Hey, Krabby!" she whispered. "There's something I see.
It's smaller than you, but it's bigger than me.
It's loping around in the tunnel, I swear!
It looked like a warthog, or maybe…a bear!"

"Don't call me 'Krabby!'" spat Mrs. Krabone,
in a violent and rather vociferous tone.
"You're a fool and a fibber!" the woman accused.
"Such ludicrous lying is never excused!"

You see, my good reader, this had happened before,
since Katrina Katrell—well, she loved to explore!

On her way home from school, whenever she could,
she would cut through a park or a forested wood;
and more often than not, in some part of a park
where no one else went until after dark,
she would see something strange, something utterly odd,
something hulking or hairy…and possibly clawed.
She then would run home, with a story to tell—
where Mrs. Krabone would do nothing but yell.

"Katrina!" she'd holler. "You ignorant thing!
Your brain must be made out of paper and string!
All this rot about yetis and monsters in lochs!
They're nothing but lies! They're nothing but crocks!"

Old Krabby, you see, was a bit of a witch.
In the pit of her heart was a serious glitch.
She didn't have time for the fanciful things,
like pirates and gadgets and creatures and kings.

She believed that a girl should be perfectly prim,
and shouldn't be guided by whimsy and whim.

As such, she was certain Katrina was nuts:
Too lively, too feisty, and too full of guts.

Yet the two were related. Yes, that much was true,
but *how* they were linked—well, nobody knew.

Their relation was distant, hard to define,
yet connected somehow by a family line,
like forty-first cousins, ten times removed
(the bloodline, however, had never been proved).

And so, once again, they had come to collide,
with each of them taking their opposite side,
as they stood near the tracks, where under the ground,
Katrina thought beasties were creeping around.

"But Krabby!" she cried. "It really is true!
It looked like a thing that escaped from a zoo!
But I'm not a dullard! And I'm not a dunce!
So you gotta believe me, if only this once!"

Mrs. Krabone said nothing at first.
Her face went all flushed, as if ready to burst.
Then her lips twisted up into sort of a grin,
and she wrangled Katrina by ear and by chin.
Leaning in close, so Katrina could hear,
she whispered maliciously into her ear:

"You listen to me. This *lying* must end.
When we get home, here is what I intend:
I will call up my friend, a Lobotomy Doc,
a talented man at the butchery block.

His scalpels are polished to shimmering shine.
He'll slice from your eye to the top of your spine.

He'll cut from your brow to the top of your head.
Your brain? He'll replace it with something instead,
something quite nice, like a pastry or cake,
or why not a succulent caribou steak?

Your original brain, he will lock in a box.
For that's what they do, those Lobotomy Docs."

Before the poor girl could swallow her fear,
Mrs. Krabone gave a tug on her ear.
So writhing and wriggling and wincing in pain,
Katrina was bullied inside of the train…

The subway struck up with its *clackity-clacks*,
rolling into the tunnel and over the tracks.

Katrina sat quietly watching the wall;
it was smeared with graffiti and scandalous scrawl.
She was searching the dark for the thing she had seen.
What was it? she thought. *What could it have been?*

At first, there was nothing that seemed out of place,
but everything changed…when she made out:

a face!

It was surely a face she would never forget.
It peered from the dark in an odd silhouette.

It wasn't a hog, or a bear, or a cat,
though perhaps if all three were stirred in a vat,
muddled and mixed into something anew:
a wildebeest, polar bear, antelope stew!

There were horns on its head, all twisty and curled;
they shot from its noggin, they spiraled and swirled.
Its shoulders, however, were stocky and stout,
and a thicket of whiskers hung down from its snout.

But perhaps the most shocking, incredible sight
she saw when the creature leaned into the light.

Not a soul would believe that it wasn't a lie,
but this creature—*this thing*—it was wearing a tie!

The train sped ahead and the shadows were back.
The creature was lost in the Stygian black.
It was gone in an instant, gone in a blink,
but not before giving Katrina... *a wink!*

She turned to her guardian, there at her side.
She was certain the truth could not be denied.

"You see now?" she said. "You can't disagree!
You looked out the very same window as me.

A creature! A thing! It was just like I said!
Perhaps there are more of them, farther ahead!"

But Mrs. Krabone was severely irate.
She spat when she spoke with fury and hate.
"A creature?!" she shrieked. "A 'mysterious beast?!'
You're crazy, Katrina, and that's saying the least!

You listen to me, you insufferable brat.
What you saw—it was probably only a rat!

So I've had quite enough! You tell me no more!
Your lies and your tales and your fibs I abhor!
If you tell me again, I shall do it myself:
I'll scoop out your brain for a spot on my shelf!"

"But didn't you see it? His horns and his beard?
And he winked I believe, which was awfully weird."

Mrs. Krabone made a shriek like a bell.

"Now you listen up,
Ms. Katrina Katrell!
I'm the boss around here! I'm your guardian, see?
Why else would your parents have sent you to me?

Well, I'll tell you why—because they know what's *best!*
That's why they made such a special request:
That *I* be the one to raise you up right!
So you'd learn to be quiet and nice and polite!

So from now on, *you pest,* you'll say not a word!
You'll say nothing silly or strange or absurd!
You'll be a good girl and you'll do what I say!
You'll shut off your mouth for
the rest of the day!"

So Katrina was silent. She made not a sound,
but her eyes remained actively darting around,

watching the weave of the wandering track,
examining close every cranny and crack,
in search of the thing that had briefly appeared,
all hairy, with horns and a whiskery beard.

A creature?

A BEASTIE?

A TROLL

or

a gnome?

But she saw nothing more,
all

the

way

home…

CHAPTER 2
a likable guy

What do you think was sneaking around, in the shadowy passages under the ground?

Katrina, of course, was thoroughly sane
(it was Mrs. Krabone who was lame in the brain).
I know this, good reader, for I can reveal:
The creature she saw—he was *perfectly real.*

If you met him yourself, that beast in the dark,
you would say, "Why, hello there!" or some such remark.
I'm certain of this. Would you like to know why?
Because Morty the zorgle's a likable guy.

A *zorgle?!* you ask. Now, don't be absurd!
A zorgle's not real! It's not even a word!
A zorgle?! What's that? you're tempted to ask.
Well, it's fine if you do, as I'm up to the task...

The zorgles are creatures fantastic and rare.
On their heads they have horns and disorderly hair.
They have pot-bellied stomachs;
their shoulders are broad;
their fingers and toes are commonly clawed.
Yet despite being fearsome in manner and mien,
the zorgles are known to be fairly serene.

They live underground, in tunnels and chutes,
in meandering caverns of tangled-up roots,
which are fed by a system of gullies and streams,
in cities like places you see in your dreams!

Now, perhaps you are thinking:
Hey, wait, what's the deal?!
A *"zorgle?!"* You're crazy! I doubt that they're real!

In that case, I ask you (and be honest please):
Would you call *observation* your top expertise?
After all, people often ignore what they see.
Just think for a moment. I'm sure you'll agree.

When someone sees something especially odd,
they assume it's a fake, or a fishy façade.
They think it's a trick of the shadows and light,
their brain playing games with their powers of sight.

The reason for this is decidedly plain:
Too often we use just a speck of our brain.
"Too busy," we say, "too tired and such.
Daydreams? Oh no, I don't use 'em so much."

So if you're a person who's tired or pooped;
if the edge of your mind has been drearily drooped,
then of course you'd ignore any zorgally face,
that perhaps you would see in some shadowy place.

So if you've no time for the whimsical things,
for pirates and gadgets and creatures and kings,

if you spurn the fantastic to never return,
then

PUT THIS BOOK DOWN...

for it's not your concern.

Ah, you're still here. Then I'm grateful to you.

(This book needs a reader, as all of them do.)

Now Mortimer Yorgle, or "Morty" for short,
was a zorgle, you see, of a singular sort.
He was certainly pleasant, and friendly enough,
but his edges, I'd say, were a little bit rough.

For instance, his necktie was always awry.
His trousers were striped with ridiculous dye.
On each of his hands he wore fingerless gloves,
and a rumpled-up raincoat was one of his loves.

His home, underground, was a humble abode:
A tumbledown hovel on *Rumbleton Road,*
in a neighborhood known to be rowdy and rough,
near the slums of a town called *Underwood Bluff.*

He worked on the staff of the newspaper crew,
at *The Underwood Telegraph Rumor Review,*
where the office was stormy with printers and ink.
They made such a racket you could hardly think!

Like a clock running wild, it's machinery broke,
the office was raging with newspaper folk,

yelling, "I've got the scoop!" or "Hold off the press!"
(How the newspaper printed was anyone's guess.)

The nature, most often, of Morty's reports
were the innings and outs of Zorgledom sports.

From judo to jousting, he covered it all,
but his favorite, of course, was *Zorgally Ball*—
an elegant game of tremendous finesse,
a cross between cricket, and swimming, and chess.

When it came to the game he was sort of a geek.
In fact, every day (or at least every week),
he would go to the stadium, take in a game,
or visit the *Ballplayer's Hallway of Fame.*

The Hallway, of course, was his favorite place.
To Morty, it harbored a mythical grace:
with its dark wooden walls, with its trophies and plaques,
with its statues of ballplayers polished in wax.

He always would pause at the end of the Hall,
where a special exhibit emblazoned the wall.
The display was an ode to his neighborhood team,
whom Morty held up in the highest esteem.

The *Underwood Titans*, that was their name.
They were commonly known as the best in the game...

Though Morty was fond of the place where he worked,
his duties were something he commonly shirked.

He often came late, not a second too soon,
and sometimes arrived at a quarter past noon!
(Which gave Porterman Shorgle, the Editor Chief,
three ulcers, gastritis, and nothing but grief).

One particular morning, when Morty blew in,
old Porterman shouted above all the din.

"Morty!" he bellowed, "you dithering dupe!
You stink! Like a heap of my goopiest poop!

Just look at the time! We're down to the crunch!
Geez, Morty, look here, it's practically lunch!"

Morty just smiled. "Well, what can I say?
I do my best work at the end of the day."

"There's no time!" cried his boss,
who was slumped in his chair,
who was nervously tugging the wisp of his hair.
He stared for a moment, not saying a word.
"Hang on," he said finally. "Haven't you heard?!"

"Heard what?" Morty asked. "I got here just now.
If I should've heard something, I'd like to know how."

Porterman scoffed in a worrying way.
"It's big news!" he exclaimed. "On the cover today!
They've all disappeared! No one knows what to do!
They've *vanished*—the zorgles of Zorgamazoo!"

"Oh, yeah," Morty said. "I've heard of that place."
A thoughtful expression passed over his face.

"Never been there myself, but my Pop's been a lot.
He explained it all once…but I've mostly forgot.
Anyhow, don't you worry. I'm sure they'll be back.
They probably got hungry, went off for a snack."

"What's the point?" said his boss, with a roll of his eyes,
with one of his patented Porterman sighs.
"You're a good writer, Mort, and that's why you're here,
but the next time you're late, you'll be out on your ear!"

Morty promised (again) to mend up his ways.
"Sure! From now on, for the rest of my days,
you'll never again have to holler and harp,
I'll be here on time, at eight o'clock sharp!"

"I hope so," said Porterman. "Start putting things right.
But for now, back to work, get outta my sight!"

So that's what he did, and as fast as he could.
But not back to work, as he'd promised he would.
Instead, Morty *left*—the same as before.
He tiptoed away and snuck out the door.

But what would make Morty go skulking away,
after coming to work so late in the day?
The answer, good reader, is just a bit sad,
and first you must get to know Mortimer's dad…

Bortlebee Yorgle, his father was called,
a little old zorgle, entirely bald,
and ever since Morty was only a tyke,
his father and he had been highly alike.

Both of them always were rumpled a bit.
Their clothes never had a particular fit.
Their gravelly voices were nearly the same,
and Zorgally Ball was their favorite game.

Yet alike as they were, they could never connect.
They differed in only a single respect:

ADVENTURE.

Adventure. That was the difference, you see,
the one thing on which they could never agree.

While Morty was known as a stick in the mud,
his Pop *loved* adventure. It was there in his blood.
Morty, however, was unlike his Pop.
When it came to adventure, he was rather a flop.

He was cut, you could say, from a different cloth,
with a nature that bordered on cowardly sloth.
Yet his father was daring. He'd wandered around
to wherever adventure was commonly found:
in the pit of a cave, on the edge of a cliff,
in search of the *how*, the *why*, the *what if?*

In his youth, he had traveled from village to town;
he had been an explorer of fame and renown.

But things change over time, as often they do,
and slowly they changed for old Bortlebee, too.
These days, he was sick. He was riddled with ills.
He was no longer known as a seeker of thrills.

He suffered, you see, from a breathing disease.
He'd wheeze and he'd sneeze until weak in the knees.
There were pains in his feet.
        There were pains in his head.
He spent most of his time in a hospital bed.
That was why Morty neglected his job,
why everyone thought he was kind of a slob,
since whenever he could, he would visit his Pop,
at *Our Lady of Zorgledom Hospital Shop.*
Together, they'd sit by the radiograph.
They'd chat about life. They'd listen and laugh.

When visiting hours would come to a close,
Morty would say: "I should go, I suppose."
Then trying to muster a smile on his face,
he would scoop up his Pop in a clumsy embrace,
knowing perfectly well that tomorrow, perhaps,
it might be the day of his father's collapse.

Yet in spite of a moment so gloomy and cold,
old Bortlebee's tone would be rosy and bold.

"I'll see ya, my son," he would merrily say.
"I'll betcha tomorrow's a beautiful day!"

When Morty got home, he'd have work to be done:
an article due that he hadn't begun!
He would sit at his typewriter, rapping the keys
while tapping his feet and bobbing his knees.
There at his desk, by the light of the moon,
he would comfort himself by humming a tune.

With a bit of a song, it was Morty's belief,
he could cope a bit better with feelings of grief.

Perhaps he was right, but here is the thing:
Late in the night, when he started to sing,
he wouldn't just whistle...he'd RATTLE *and* **ROLL**!
His singing would often fly out of control.

So his neighbors would holler: "Hey, quit it, ya creep!
You're singing off-key, and we're trying to sleep!"

So he might settle down. He might even stop,
but he still would be troubled with thoughts of his Pop.
Yet somehow he'd finish, alone in the night,
he'd work until darkness was turning to light…

I am utterly certain, without any doubt,
it would've kept going, day in and day out,
if it weren't for events that would alter his plan,
on the day his amazing *adventure* began…

But for now, my good reader, the greetings are done.
The story of Mortimer Yorgle's begun.
The moment has come to move onward and find:

Katrina and Morty—

their fates
are
entwined...

CHAPTER 3
the lobotomy doc

We now
shall return to Katrina Katrell,
who was feeling unhappy and rather unwell.
She had sadly been locked in her bedroom alone,
by the hand of her guardian, Mrs. Krabone.

Perhaps the one question you're anxious to know
is regarding her parents: *Like, where did they go?*
Well, in stories like these, as I'm sure you have read,
the parents, quite often, are thoroughly dead:
run over by rhinos or gored by a moose,
or murdered when somebody poisoned their juice.

In this case, however, I'm sorry to say,
her parents weren't dead, they were merely...*away*.

They were wealthy, you see. They were captains of trade,
adept in the ways in w hich money was made.
So they traveled *a lot*, a tremendous amount
(while charging it all to a corporate account).

Theirs was a world of banking and loans,
of virtual meetings and cellular phones;
of foreign investment and business affairs;
of taxis and boardrooms and leathery chairs.

All of their life was spent up in the air,
incessantly flying from here and to there.
From Lisbon to London, from Paris to Rome,
they had gone off on business, and never come home.

Why, even Katrina was born on the fly,
on a company jet that was up in the sky.
Her mother, of course, was under-prepared.
"A baby?! How awkward!" the woman declared.

"I haven't got time for raising a kid,
and I doubt that I'd want to, if even I did!"

When her father got word that Katrina was born,
he grimaced a little and got on the horn.
He called his accountant to raise a concern:
"On *babies,*" he asked, "what's the rate of return?"

So you see, my good reader, her parents were duds.
Too much of the blue in the both of their bloods.

This was the reason Katrina was thrown
together with "Mrs. Gremelda Krabone,"
which of course made Katrina abundantly glum,
to be languishing under her guardian's thumb.

It's not fair! she was thinking.
It's simply not right!
Being locked in my room without dinner tonight!
Such were the thoughts that were filling her head,
as she hungrily hunched on the edge of her bed.
But just as her anger was reaching its peak,
from the silence below, came an ominous creeeeeeeeaak!

Katrina was puzzled. She thought, with a frown:
Who would be calling to this part of town?
A prowler, perhaps, or a murderer might.
Who else would come visit so late in the night?

She climbed to her knees, with an ear to the floor.
With her hands on the carpet, she listened for more.
From below came an almost inaudible drone,
but she knew who it was by its nasally tone...

Old Krabby?! she thought, in a logical leap.
Right now the old bat should be snoring asleep!
Yet Old Krabby was up! She was talking as well.
But why and to whom?! thought Katrina Katrell.

It was then she recalled what Old Krabby had said,
and what she was planning to do with her head!
Could it really be true?! Was she being sincere?!
She'd invited some wacko and now...*he was here?!*

Katrina stood up. It would likely be best
to break out of her room on a miniature quest.
She would snoop just a bit, go sneaking around.
She would sort out the source of this mystery sound...

She pulled up the carpet, where no one would look,
revealing an almost invisible nook;
and there in the dark was a treasury trunk
filled with a clutter of jumble and junk.

Most people would think it was nothing but fluff,
a collection of doodads and whatchamastuff.
To Katrina, however, one thing was true:
This stuff came in handy—you just never knew.

She dug up a spring from a grandfather clock…
It was just the right thingy to *jimmy a lock!*

She twisted the spring and she made it a key
(she was rather inventive, I'm sure you can see).
Then gripping the spring in her sensitive fist,
she opened the latch with a flick of her wrist.

Then quietly pacing with caution and care,
she crept down the hall to the top of the stair;
and down a few steps, like a gossamer ghost,
she peered 'round a lopsided banister post…

A man stood below, on the entranceway mat,
his collar turned up to the brim of his hat.
He took off his gloves, his cap, and his coat.
He loosened the muffler that covered his throat.

His features were drawn and incredibly dark,
but his eyes were aglow with a sinister spark.

Old Krabby was there. She was wringing her hands,
like a criminal, hatching felonious plans.

She quietly spoke to the man in the hall:
"Doctor, I'm glad you could answer my call.
It's nice you could visit so late in the night,
I'm certain your skill will set everything right!
You'll cut out the naughtiest bits of her brain,
so only the parts that are normal remain."

"I will do what I can," the stranger replied,
"your need for a surgeon cannot be denied;
because Madam, your case is a serious one.
So let us discuss it. Just what's to be done?"

Above, in the stairwell, Katrina was still,
her fingers and throat in the grip of a chill.
This stranger, she sensed, by his timbre and tone,
was the sort to send shivers that shook to the bone.

Now, here's what Katrina so furtively heard,
as her guardian spoke in a whispering word:

"It's my girl. She's upstairs, and she's coming unwound.
Why, she's quite a few ounces short of a pound!
Delusions of grandeur, that's what she's got!
She thinks she's so special! She thinks she's so hot!

She thinks of herself as courageous and brave,
but doctor, I wish she would simply behave!
But her brain is **diseased**, it's gone on the blink!
She's completely insane! She's right on the brink!

Why, only today she redoubled my doubt
by claiming some creature was skulking about.
Some sort of a beastie, with horns on its head,
and wearing a tie! Or that's what she *said*..."

As he listened, the Doctor was thumbing his case,
Silent and solemn and gazing in space.
His brow furrowed up like a fisherman's knot,
and cried, "We must strike while the iron is hot!

Her condition is worse than at first I'd assumed,
so we mustn't delay, or else she is doomed!
It is clear to me now that certainly she's:
got Parapsychotic Delusion Disease!

There is only one method to fix it within...
which I'll demonstrate now, before I begin."

He opened his bag with imperious pride,
and Katrina saw horrible things were inside:
needles and skewers that filled her with fright,
as they glinted and shone in the shadowy light.

The doctor reached deep in his medical case,
and took out a tool too gruesome to face.
It looked like a drill, but especially made,
with clappers and claws and a rotary blade!

He fondled this *thing*, with the subtlest touch.
"I love it!" he cried. "Oh, ever so much!
It's the finest, most delicate tool of its kind.
It's the

Cranial Puncturing Mincer of Mind!

And if you'll excuse some innocuous fun,
I'll demonstrate now how the mincing is done!"

He spun on his heel, and he leapt in the air,
recalling the cadence of Freddy Astaire,
but never as nimble, not nearly as spry
(more like a hippo with mud in its eye).
He leaped and he danced with his terrible tool!
He flourished and spun like a blathering fool!

"Madam," he puffed, when his dancing was done,
"In the surgical world, I am second to none!
So you've nothing to fear, for I'll snip off her top.
I flip up her lid and I'll give her *the chop!*"

But Old Krabby was bored. She looked up at the clock.
She was eager to get to the butchery block.

"Doctor LeFang," she said, with a smile,
"I don't mean to rush you or hamper your style,
but perhaps we should start by moving upstairs.
It's best if Katrina is... *caught unawares.*
It's not that your banter is dreary or dull,
it's just that I'm anxious to crack at her skull!"

They both looked above at the balcony ledge,
but Katrina already had left from the edge.
She had scampered away and back to her bed,
trembling with panic and dizzy with dread.

It would seem she was caught in a bit of a scrape,
and the only way out was to stage an escape!
So she packed up a sack, full of clothing and socks,
and much of the junk from her treasury box.

Then she tied up her sheets in a delicate line,
like Tarzan would do with a tropical vine;
one end she tied to the foot of her bed,

while the other she tossed out the window, instead.

Then she leapt out herself, swung down on the sheets,
repelling below, to the dark of the streets.

While up in her bedroom, Old Krabby was there,
ranting and raving and tearing her hair.
She had searched all the rooms, from hither to yon,
and discovered Katrina was thoroughly gone.

She howled with a shriek that was bitter and shrill.
It was just as the doctor leaned over the sill.
"Look! Out the window!" he said with a scoff,
"...I wonder why all of my patients run off?"

Mrs. Krabone cried: "Don't mess around!
We can catch her again if we get to the ground!"

She wrangled the doctor away by his cuff,
and they sped down the stairs in a tumbling huff.
But when they arrived at the base of the stair,
Katrina was gone—by barely a hair!
She had fled! She was free! (Not a moment too soon.)

She had scampered away, by the light of the moon!
Yes, she'd escaped, when the timing was right,
but what dangers awaited, out there, in the night?

Meanwhile, Old Krabby was red as a beet.
She was gnashing her teeth! She was stomping her feet!
She clutched at the collar of Doctor LeFang,
subjecting the man to a hairy harangue:

"You listen to me,
you incompetent
quack!
If it wasn't for you and your yakkety-yak,
I'd have my Katrina now under the knife.
She would finally give me some peace in my life!

But instead of my peace, as I'm sure you can guess,
I get only a lousy, lamentable mess!
So listen up good, you botchery buff!
You bungler! You dunce! You pandering puff!
May it take us a week! Or a month! Or a year!

We will find my Katrina, and *bring her back here!*
Then using that miserable 'Mincer of Mind,'
you'll finish the job that you were assigned!"

So Mrs. Krabone (and the Doctor, as well),
began searching the streets for Katrina Katrell.
They scoured the ground. They hunted and hoped.
They rummaged and rooted and grabbled and groped.

They sniffed with their noses. They narrowed their eyes.
They even looked up to the dark of the skies.
They listened as well, but heard nothing at all...

just the flap
of the sheets
that hung from the wall.

CHAPTER 4
a fluttering flame

With Katrina,
her story began with a leap,
eluding LeFang—that nefarious creep.

Mortimer's story was hardly the same.
It began with a sort of a lottery game…
A game with a prize that was *truly* bizarre:
Not a nifty new house or a nimble new car.
Not the tastiest meal or the fanciest clothes.
A prize that was nothing like any of those.

Not boodle, not moolah, not money or gold,
or anything else you could handle or hold.

What sort of prize could it possibly be?
Read on, my good reader, and soon you will see…

It was late in the night, in Underwood Bluff,
as Morty tramped home in a bit of a huff.
All day he had toiled at the *Rumor Review*,
at a legion of deadlines, soon to be due.

So staggering home, he was bleary and beat.
He was sluggish and slow. He was dragging his feet.
There was only one thought in the whole of his head:
To find his way home and to climb into bed.

But he couldn't quite yet. He still had to stop
and check on his Pop in the Hospital Shop.

It was then something happened: a scent on the breeze.
It blew up his nose and he thought he would sneeze.
The odor was acrid. The odor was hot—
like a casserole burning inside of a pot.

It tickled the whiskers that grew in his nose.
He stopped in his tracks. He suddenly froze.

Holy smokes! Morty thought. *A fire?! But where?!*
He snuffled and followed the smell in the air.
It led him away, to the end of the block,
where Mortimer Yorgle was in for a shock...

There stood the Ballplayers Hallway of Fame.
It glimmered within with
a fluttering flame!

"Oh, no!" Morty cried, with a panicky yelp.
"The Hallway! It's burning! Hey, somebody! *HELP!*"
He ran in a circle and waggled his arms.
"Hurry!" he hollered. "Sound the alarms!"

But no one came running to Mortimer's aid.
He was all by himself, completely dismayed!
For here was his favorite place in the world,
going up in a fire that flickered and swirled.

Feeling woozy, he wobbled and fell to the ground.
No one was coming. There was no one around.

He thought of the trophies, the statues and plaques,
melting in puddles of silver and wax;
and all of that history—all of it lost!
It had to be saved! No matter the cost!

It was then, to his horror, that Mortimer knew,
there was only one thing he could possibly do.
He couldn't just sit there, he couldn't just wait.
He'd been poked...by the ficklest finger of fate!

(But Morty and fate were like water and oil:
From the latter, the former would always recoil.)
So Morty did nothing. He slumped and he stared,
while firelight sizzled and fizzled and flared.

Why me?! Morty thought. *I'm just a chump!*
I'm a rube! I'm a clod! I'm a sap! I'm a frump!
Where are the sirens? Where are the lights?
On this, the most terrible night of all nights?!
And what if, perhaps, they just never came?
Would it burn to a crisp—The Hallway of Fame?!

The answer, of course, was a definite: *Yes!*
There'd be nothing left but a smoldering mess.

And for even a chump that was easy to see.
Aw, crud, Morty thought. *It's all up to me…*

He got to his feet, his heart full of dread.
He pulled up his trench coat over his head.
He looked at a window that rippled with heat,
and willed himself forward on faltering feet.

Then faster and faster! A blundering dash!
He dove through the glass with a clattering **smash!**

Inside of the building, the walls were ablaze.
The smoke in the air was a murderous haze.
Everything blossomed with yellows and reds,
braided together in fiery threads.

It felt like the heat was a million degrees!
So Morty got down on his hands and his knees.

Bewildered and aimless, he started to crawl
the length of that lofty, illustrious hall,
randomly grabbing whatever he could:
trinkets of plastic and metal and wood.

He wormed to the end, where the heat was the worst,
his mouth going dry as if dying of thirst.
There, behind glass, in an elegant chest,
was a relic more precious than all of the rest:

A zorgally ball that once had been flung
by Cyril "The Slinger" Zipzorgle DeYoung,
in the very first Underwood Champions Match,
when balls were still woven from ravels of thatch.

Morty opened the case and plucked up the ball,
as the fire was rising to swallow the Hall,
abruptly erupting in flashes and blooms,
imbuing the room with its poisonous fumes!

It was then Morty knew: The time was at hand
to blow this proverbial popsicle stand!

But he hardly could see! The smoke was too dense!
The heat all around him was more than intense!
He snaked on his belly and made for the door,
through inches of ashes that covered the floor.

He might well have made it, but started to choke,
inhaling a lungful of cindery smoke.

All at once he was weak, he was gasping for breath.
He was two or three breaths from the edges of death!

His stomach was churning. His vision was blurred.
If you said: *"He's a goner!"* I would've concurred.
But then he heard something: A series of *thwacks,*
like the chopping of wood with the crack of an axe.
And then something else: the tromping of boots,
from zorgles in bulky, voluminous suits.

They stood around Morty, who lay like a log,
whose senses were fuzzy and lost in a fog.
But before passing out, he was never afraid,
for the boots…
they belonged to the fire brigade.

When Morty awoke, he was tucked in a bed,
an uncomfortable pillow supporting his head.

In the room where he was, the lighting was bright;
the walls and the ceiling were blindingly white.

He smiled to himself. He was hardly surprised.
How ironic, he thought, *I've been hospitalized.*
He looked down at himself and instinctively cringed.
He was covered in cuts. His hair had been singed.

I'm a loser, he thought. *I'm a dough-headed klutz!*
What was I thinking?! I must've been nuts!

"Welcome back!" said a voice. It was gruff, like his own,
and Mortimer realized he wasn't alone.
He rolled to his left and there was his Pop.
They were sharing a room at the Hospital Shop.

"Hi, Pop," Morty said. "I screwed-up, I guess.
Just look at me here! I'm a terrible mess!"

"Screwed-up?" said his Pop. He was taken aback.
A part of him wished to give Morty a smack.
"But I *love* what you did! Sounds like it was fun!
And you know what they say—like father, like son!"

"Yeah, right." Morty scoffed. "Maybe *you* think it's cool,
but I'm aching all over. I feel like a fool.
I haven't felt *this* bad since—I dunno when!
I'll never do something that stupid again!"

"Ssshhh!" said his Pop, as he nodded his head
to the stranger who stood at the end of the bed:
A respectable zorgle, impeccably dressed
in a Chesterfield cloak and a cardigan vest.

"Who're you?" Morty squinted. "When'd you arrive?
I don't need an embalmer, 'cause I'm still alive."

The stranger said nothing to Mortimer's joke.
He reached with a hand in the folds of his cloak.
He came out with a document wound in a roll,
an archaic and rather elaborate scroll.

The stranger unfurled it. It flapped to his feet.
The inscription was lush and exquisitely neat.

"Dear sir,"

he recited, beginning to read
the document's pompous, punctilious screed.
"On behalf of the BUREAU OF HEROES
AND QUESTS,
we acknowledge your deed, which plainly attests
to your selflessness, bravery, vigor and verve,
as well as your steely, unwavering nerve.

Thanks to your efforts in tackling the blaze,
we can rebuild the Hall and its many displays!
Such spirited courage should not be ignored,
which is why we confer you this noble reward..."

The stranger then paused, leaning over the bed.
He held out his fist and momentously said:
"To Mortimer Yorgle, of Rumbleton Road,
his *lottery ticket* is humbly bestowed!"

The ticket was crimson, its lettering blue,
saying:

We Need a Hero, and Maybe It's **You**!

When Mortimer read it, he said with a smile,
"I think that I'll pass. This isn't my style.

I know how this works. I know what you do.
You send people off to run errands for you.
But it's usually terrible, dangerous stuff.
And the both of us know—it's nothing but guff!
'Cause you make it seem noble and daring and cool.
But you're not duping me! I'm nobody's fool!

In this game the winner does nothing but *lose.*
They won't come back alive—whoever you choose!
So honestly, sir, I would *love* to comply.
But a 'hero?' Not me. You got the wrong guy."

"No! I think not!" the stranger replied.
"The selection is hardly for *you* to decide!
Why, this is an honor! A privilege, sir!
You cannot decline and you cannot defer!

You haven't a choice! You will come to Draw,
in accordance with Zorgledom Chivalry Law!"

The stranger gave Morty the shallowest bow.
"You hereby are hero material now."
Then he turned on his heels and turned up his nose,
and he left with his scroll and his marvelous clothes.

"Fat chance!" Morty called. "Like I'm gonna go!
I won't be some stooge in a lottery show!"
But then, when he turned and he looked at his Pop,
the old guy was grinning—he just couldn't stop.

"Just imagine!" he said. "To be given the chance,
to rescue the world, by the seat of your pants!
That's what it means to be chosen, you see,
and if I was still young…they might've picked me."
Old Bortlebee seemed to have stars in his eyes.
"Aw, Morty!" he mooned. "What a wonderful prize!"

"Well, sure," Morty said. "Maybe for *you.*
But what if I won? I don't know what I'd do."
From his pillow, old Bortlebee lifted his head.
"We're different. I know that," he quietly said.

"But look at me here. I'm sick to the core.
Each morning I'm worse than the morning before."

He gazed at his son, looked him right in the eye.
"It's true: Someday soon I will probably die.
Before then, I want you, my one only son,
to have *an adventure*...and maybe some fun!

I know your chances—well, they're not very good.
You likely won't win, but just maybe *you could.*
So think of this thing as my ultimate hope.
My one last request...at the end of my rope."

For a moment, Morty said nothing at all.
He looked out the window, and then at the wall.
He looked at his Pop, who seemed thoroughly drained,
whose expression was hopeful, yet equally pained.

Then Morty looked down at the slip in his hand.
"I'll do it," he nodded. "But I don't understand...
The *details,* they seem just a little bit thin.
Like the actual prize—what will I win?"

Old Bortlebee angled his mouth in a smile.
The answer, he said, would come in a while...

CHAPTER 5
the lottery draw

The following night, by the Underwood Mall,
at the Zorgledom Central Community Hall,
a billboard was posted, inspiring awe:
Welcome, it said, *to the Lottery Draw!*

Hundreds of zorgles awaited inside.
They came from all points, from far and from wide.
Muscular zorgles, zorgles of might,
zorgles renowned to be good in a fight.

There was also a stage and an orchestra band—
who started to play! The show was at hand!

The curtains rose up and everyone cheered.
Before them was something stupendously weird:
A **contraption** like nothing that
you've ever seen:
An incredibly intricate marble machine!

It bristled with pulleys and spiraling tracks,
suspended with rivets and wire and wax;

with miniature bridges, with pillars and piers;
with levers and winches and clutches and gears;
with pedals and treadles and spinners and spars;
with pendulous pivots and balancing bars;
with motors and rotors and rollers and ramps;
with flickering bulbs and electrical lamps;
with flingers and swingers and hinges and hubs;
with grabbers and funnels and buckets and tubs;
with clockwork propellers, mechanical cranks,
and panels and chimneys and channels and planks!

Nobody spoke.
Who there would dare?
An odd sort of peace had come into the air.

The host of the night, the Lottery Boss,
leapt up on the stage and sauntered across.
A plump little fellow, this captain of chance,
who twitched like his jacket was crawling with ants.

"Good evening!" he bellowed. "Welcome, as well!
Are you anxious to start? You are, I can tell!
This machine, as you know, just off to my rear
is the reason you've come. It's the reason we're here!
And *what* a machine! Why, isn't it nice?
It's the *Hero Selection Divining Device*!"

Everyone clapped. They hollered and cheered.
All except Morty. He was scratching his beard.

The Lottery Boss, he waited until
the crowd, once again, was quiet and still.

"Your names," he went on, "are within the machine.
They're written on marbles—*nine hundred nineteen!*

When I yank on the lever that's here at my side,
the nine hundred marbles will go for a ride.

They will enter the funnel that starts at the top,
they will tumble and roll 'til they come to a stop;
because only one marble will finally roll
to the end, to the base, to the *Destiny Bowl!*"

The "Destiny Bowl" was more like a flask;
it was heavy and broad, like a barrel or cask.
On its side was a letter, which Morty could see
was written in rubies—a big letter

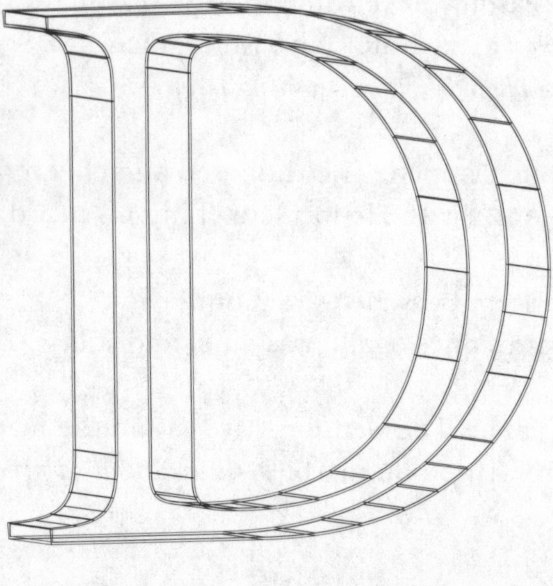

“Wait!” Morty called. “Before we begin?
You still haven’t said what the winner will win!”

The Lottery Boss tipped the brim of his hat.
“Well, of course!” he exclaimed. “I was getting to that.
You see, my good friends, there’s adventure ahead!
Perhaps you have read what the newspaper said.
The countryside zorgles have all disappeared!
They were lost in the night, or so it is feared!

So the winner tonight wins a compass, a map,
a flashlight, galoshes, a coat and a cap,
to help with the search, when the going is rough!
…plus all kinds of other adventuring stuff!

And then something better than all else combined!
An expenses-paid trip to head out there and find
the zorgles who vanished with nary a clue:
those countryside zorgles of Zorgamazoo!”

To Morty, this sounded like less of a prize,
and more like a punishment put in disguise.

But there wasn't much time to consider for long,
for the orchestra started performing a song,
and the Lottery Boss went over to stand
in the place where the lever awaited his hand.

"Now remember," he said, "that in any event,
this machine is correct, one hundred percent!
It will magically choose from this clamoring mob
the most suitable zorgle for doing the job!"

He beamed at the crowd with his simpering grin.
"Now! Let the lottery raffle begin!"
With his hand on the lever, he gave it a push,
and the marbles came down with a

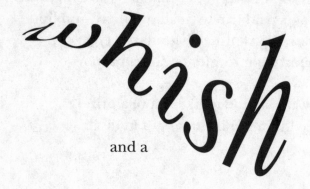

whish

and a

whosh

Then into the funnel
and onto the tracks,

down through the rivets

and wire and wax,

guided by channels and panels and planks,

battered and clanged in mechanical cranks,

over

the motors and rotors and ramps,

under the glow of electrical lamps,

c r o s s i n g

the miniature bridges and piers,

rolling and reeling in winches and gears,

s p i r a l i n g down along spinners and spars,

bouncing between all the balancing bars,

flung by the flingers and into the hubs,

caught in the catchers and

funnels and tubs...

Then, when the running was finally done,
with odds that were more than nine hundred-to-one,
a particular marble was down at the goal.
Alone, on its own, in the *Destiny Bowl.*

The Lottery Boss, he skipped and he hopped,
to the bowl on the floor, where that marble had stopped.

He plucked it right up and read what it said.
Then he paused.
And he frowned.
And he waggled his head.

"Fancy that," he said softly. "I suppose this is right!
Where's *'Mortimer Y?'* He's our winner tonight!"

All of the zorgles were looking around
to see if this "Mortimer Y." could be found.
Mortimer knew they were looking for him.
He had won, though the odds were incredibly slim.

It can't be, he thought, *they've made a mistake!*
He was suddenly woozy and started to shake.

His palms were all clammy; he thought he would faint.
For he was no hero, no idol, no saint!
He was just Morty, just Morty the hack,
and he sensed he was having a panic attack.

But then he remembered his desperate dad,
whose illness was growing increasingly bad.
He thought of his Pop in that hospital bed,
swaddled in gauze from his hips to his head…

So in spite of reluctance, confusion, and fear,
the thoughts in his head were surprisingly clear.

He planted his feet.
He started to rise.
He went to the stage,
and collected his prize…

Back at the hospital, Bortlebee lay,
musing about the events of the day.

His mind was befuddled with thoughts of his son,
wishing and hoping that Morty had won.

So when Morty arrived, with a map in his hand,
charting the course to a faraway land,
old Bortlebee smiled. He instantly knew:
his incredible dream was incredibly true!

"Well," Morty croaked, with a lump in his throat.
"They gave me this map, plus a cap and a coat.
It's awful! I won! As you probably guessed.
So they're sending me off on some sort of a quest.
But I'm not the right guy," he fretfully said.
"I'm telling you, Pop, I'm in over my head!"

"Don't be a scaredy-cat," Bortlebee teased.
"Can't you see that I'm happy? I'm terribly pleased!
Just do it for me and wipe off the frown.
Be happy! For once you'll get out of this town."

He looked at his son, and uttered a sigh.
It was time, he could see, for saying goodbye.

"I hope," he said slowly, "you have nothing but luck.
But remember: Whenever you're stuck in the muck,
when the travels are rough and you're stuck up a tree,
you remember this, Morty: You've always got me."

"Aw, Pop," Morty grumbled. "I love ya, too.
And that's why I'm going. I'll do it for you."

Then they hugged one another, especially tight,
and Morty set off, that very same night…

CHAPTER 6
the *gang* of mccrook

n the surface above, in the world that you know,

Katrina Katrell was a girl on the go.
But where was she headed? She hadn't a clue.
She just had to keep going—it was all that she knew.

Yet a terrible rain was flooding the streets,
falling in thundering, merciless sheets.
Katrina was soaked. She was practically drowned,
but she had to escape. She couldn't be found.

For Mrs. Krabone was hot on her trail,
tracking her down, by tooth and by nail;
and with her that lunatic, Doctor LeFang,
who would mince up her mind into lemon meringue!

What she needed was shelter, some haven or place,
to escape from the chill and the rain and the chase.

It was then
          that she spotted a place she could hide:
at the end of an alley, off to the side,
a hatch in the wall that might be a door,
or an entrance that wasn't in use anymore.

On the wall near the hatch was a kind of sign.
It was hung on the brick with some raggedy twine.
The words on the placard were SLOPPY and wild,
as if scrawled by the hand of an ignorant child.

Yet this was a sign that was meant to be read,
and these are the words that it messily said:

Hey you! That's right—you! Hoo-ever you are,
from down on the korner or kountries afar,
we don't give a fig abowt who you mite be!
So leev us alone! And go leep in the sea!

(And then, if you still hav a sekund to spare,
then you mite as well drown, fer all that we care!)

Cuz to us, you're a dogg, and you're way off yer leesh!
So beat it, OK? SKEDADDLE! *Kapeesh?*
You still wanna come in? Well, you're badly mistook,
cuz you don't wanna mess with the
Gang of McCrook!

The alley, however, was terribly dim;
the rain was so thick you could go for a swim;
the wind was a billowy, blustery gust,
and the placard was grubby and covered with rust.

So Katrina, of course, didn't notice the sign.
She assumed that the doorway was perfectly fine.

She splashed to the handle and waggled the latch,
and to her surprise...that opened the hatch.
Inside was a ladder, with rungs in a row,
a stairway of steps to a chamber below.

But the stairway was crooked, the ladder was cracked
(on the verge of collapse, as a matter of fact).
Descending the stairway, its pilasters shook,
they wobbled and quaked like a fish on a hook.

At the bottom, the walls were discolored and bare,
and shadows, like spirits, were haunting the air.

Looking around, Katrina could see:
a booth, where you once put a ticketing fee,
some rusty old tracks for an underground train,
and maps from the past to explain the terrain.
Seeing it all, she could fairly deduce:
This was a station...no longer in use.

At this point, Katrina was terribly bushed;
she couldn't go on, even if she were pushed.
She needed a dwelling for resting her head,
a comfortable place she could set for a bed.

After some searching, she spotted a room,
that wasn't too buried in rubbish and gloom.
She lay on the floor, on a pillow of stone,
feeling wretched, dejected, completely alone.

But just as she readied herself for a doze,
just as her eyes were beginning to close,
just as she started to slumber and snooze,
she was jolted awake by the *thrumping* of shoes!

"Well, well!" came a voice like the squeal of a saw.
"It looks like some joker has broken the law!
Perhaps not a *certified* law of the land,
but for sure—it's the only law *we* understand.

"Now what sorta law am I talking about?
The law that says:

EVERYONE BETTER
KEEP OUT!"

Katrina looked up from her place in the scruffs.
She was cornered, she saw, by a trio of toughs!
Two boys and a girl who were older than she,
a dirty, despicable, criminal three!

The girl was in gumboots as tall as a chair.
She had daggers and knives pinned up in her hair.
Her name on the street was
"Selena the Slash,"
and she'd cut off your pants to pilfer your cash!

To her left was an impish and rascally scamp,
dressed in the rags of a traveling tramp.
His nickname was "Sickly" or
"SICKLY VAN PUKE"
and his nose always trickled with gobbledygook.

The last was a ruffian lofty and tall,
as strong as an ox and as wide as a wall,
with a look on his face, so purple and mean—
like a face you might make in a stinky latrine.

Katrina concluded with only a look
this last was none other than

BUGSY McCROOK!

(Now the Gang of McCrook was a miserable mob,
for whom robbing you blind was an everyday job.

They were known for their violence and criminal feats,
for a seedy selection of sinful deceits—
from robbery, arson, and pyramid schemes,
to snatching the mascots from basketball teams.

They had once robbed a pet shop of all of its cash,
and they never—*not ever*—recycled their trash!)

"I know who you are," Katrina exclaimed.
"You're **BUGSY McCROOK**, and you should be ashamed!"

"At your service," said **BUGSY**. He bent in a bow.
"I wonder, my dear, what *shall* we do now?"

"I know!" said **the girl** in the cumbersome boots,
"Let's force-feed her full of some festering fruits!

We can sting her with bees as much as we please!
We can scrape up her knees with a grater of cheese!
We can jab her with sticks, and if she survives,
That's fine! Then we'll *stick* her with one of my knives!"

SICKLY agreed with insidious glee.
"You're a genius, Selena, that's easy to see!
She must've been blind, ignoring our sign!
We'll force her to whinny and whimper and whine!"

"Wait!" said Katrina. "Hold on for a sec.
Before you go crazy, start wringing my neck,
before you begin to dissever and maim,
hold on—at least let me tell you my name."

"Alright," **BUGSY** sneered, "but get on with it, see.
Then you'll get your shellacking,
and you'll get it from me!"
Katrina raised up her adorable head.
She smiled like an angel, and here's what she said:

"They call me Katrina,

Katrina Katrell

and I hope you all fall down a bottomless well."

Then, like a cat, she sprung to her feet.
She spun on her heels, to beat a retreat.

As she scuttled away, she was granted a chance
to give SICKLY a kick in the seat of his pants.

Selena she tripped with a flick of her foot
which made her go sprawling in rubble and soot.

But then, at the steps, before her escape,
she was captured by someone as strong as an ape!

It was **BUGSY McCROOK!** He was already there!
He hoisted her up by a handful of hair!

Katrina looked back at her turbulent wake:
Selena lay sprawled like a slumbering snake.
Her boots were askew and her hair was a mess.
There were tatters and tears in her leathery dress.

SICKLY, meanwhile, was especially glum.
He was sulking and sourly rubbing his bum.

"Okay," **BUGSY** puffed, "we're skipping the bees.
You can nix all the sticks and the grater of cheese.
Instead, I've decided to skip to the punch.
Let's finish her off, get down to the crunch.

"Ms. Katrina Katrell, say goodbye to your life,
because now, as we say, is *the time of the knife!*"

Selena provided her terrible blade.
It flashed like the games in a penny arcade.
She gave it to **BUGSY**, who grinned like a shark,
whose teeth were agleam in the shadowy dark.
But before he could act on his odious goals,
before he could riddle Katrina with holes,

he was stopped by a voice that rose from the gloom,
and suddenly rippled all over the room.

The voice started whistling a musical tune,
like a wolf, as it croons at the sight of a moon.
While yowling a jingle and clapping a beat,
the whistler was happily tapping his feet.

The tapping grew louder, just off to the right,
and then Mortimer Yorgle…

tripped into the light.

"Excuse me," he coughed. "I got carried away.
It happens sometimes. Hey, what can I say?"

BUGSY looked frightened. Or startled, at least,
as he gaped at this creature, this blundering beast.

"Hello," Morty waved. "I don't mean to intrude.
I hope you'll excuse me for being so rude.
But I got myself lost," he said with remorse.
"I don't know where I am. I'm a little off course."

BUGSY said nothing, he just ogled and stared.
The pigheaded bully was actually scared!

His lips began trembling, he started to pout.
He tried saying *something*, but nothing came out,
nothing except for a meaningless peep,
the teeniest, tiniest, whiniest...

"eep!"

The knife in his hand, it fell to the floor,
and **BUGSY MCCROOK** ran off for the door.

His minions, Selena and SICKLY VAN PUKE,
(whose nose was now *gushing* with gobbledygook),
they were equally scared. They ran away, too.
Up the stairwell they scampered—they practically flew!

So Katrina was left, alone with this *thing*,
not knowing what dangers their meeting would bring.
But running away—well, it didn't seem right,
after Morty had proved himself rather polite.

So she put out her hand. It hung there a while.
On her face was a grateful but timorous smile.

"My name's Katrina, and I'd just like to say:
Thank you—for going so out of your way.
Those ruffians sure had me under the knife,
so I owe it to you…for saving my life."

Morty reached out, with the palm of his paw.
They shook, and Katrina was stricken with awe.

"Who me?" Morty asked. "You got me all wrong.
I was just passing through, just humming a song."

His hand and his fingers were far from the norm.
They were furry
                    and roughened
          and toughened
                    and warm.

"Pleased to meet you," he said. "I'm Morty, or 'Mort.'
To be honest, I'm not the adventuring sort.
But they sent me, it seems, on a sort of a quest,
and I've got myself lost…and I'm sort of depressed.
And there's no one to help me!" he said with a sigh,
as he awkwardly straightened the knot of his tie.

The tie! thought Katrina. It was perfectly plain!
It was *him*—the same face she had seen on the train!

"You're the thing that I saw!" She let out a squeal.
"I can hardly believe that you're actually real!"
Morty looked at Katrina. He furrowed his brow.
"Oh yeah, on the train. I remember you now."

That's how it began, as simple as that!
Soon they were chatting and chewing the fat.
And Katrina could see, in Mortimer's eye,
that here was a decent and likable guy.

They spoke of their lives, above and below,
recounting their personal stories of woe.
Katrina endeavoured to try and explain
the insidious perils besetting her brain.

How Mrs. Krabone had commissioned a quack,
to pry at her skull with a *crick* and a *crack!*

Morty meanwhile—he spoke of his quest,
his lottery ticket, and all of the rest.
He mentioned his Pop, who was sick as a dog,
who sagged in his bed like a moldering log.

But mostly he griped about being picked,
how to him it appeared as if he'd been tricked.
"What a joke!" he lamented. "I haven't a *clue*
how to find any zorgles in Zorgamazoo!"

As she listened, Katrina was greatly engrossed.
This tale had the stuff she admired the most:
a potential adventure, with thrill after thrill!
She soaked it all up. She was utterly still.

But her belly had butterflies flitting inside.
Her breathing had quickened. Her eyes had gone wide.
She felt like her body was lit from within.
On her face, was the subtlest hint of a grin.

And so, it was then that Katrina Katrell
decided to have an adventure as well…

"Listen," she said. "I don't mean to pry,
but I'd sure like to give an adventure a try.
I always wanted to travel, to ramble and roam,
but old Krabby won't let me. She keeps me at home.
So this is my chance, I'm off on my own.
I can travel the world! Explore the unknown!"

Morty thought for a moment. He paced in a loop.
He went moping around in a sort of a stoop.
"Wait a second," he said. "Are you actually sure?
If you join me, who knows what we'll have to endure. . ."

"Of course!" said Katrina. "I could give you a hand.
I could help you to make it to Zorgamaland.
I'm good with a map and I'm quick on my feet.
Who knows? Perhaps we were destined to meet!"

Morty chuckled and smiled. "Okay, you can stop.
You know, you remind me a bit of my Pop.
He's nothing like me. He's all gutsy, like you.
Oh, and one other thing: It's 'Zorgama*zoo*.'"

"Fair enough," said Katrina. "Now hand me the map."
Which he did, and she opened it up in her lap.

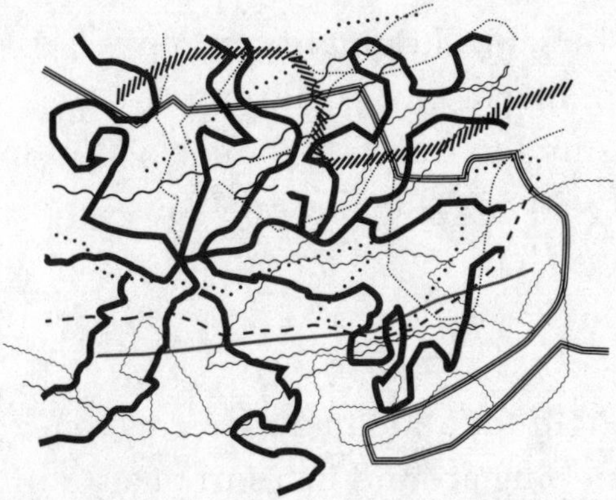

Every inch of the paper was covered with roads,
with passages, tunnels and curious codes.
It seemed to be utterly puzzling at first.
In no time Katrina was deeply immersed.

Then, all at once, it seemed to make sense,
despite being so inextricably dense.
"I've got it!" she said. "It's all coming clear.
There should be a doorway. . .

right

over

here."

She pointed across to a cleft in the wall,
a gap that was hardly a doorway at all.
It led to a tunnel, forbidding and dark:
the path onto which they were set to embark.

As they vanished inside and into the black
Katrina knew then:

There was
no turning back…

CHAPTER 7
the tunnel of *hush*

It seemed like they traveled for several days, through a network of tunnels, an intricate maze.

The tunnel was twisty. It angled around,

through hundreds of passages
under the ground.

Going farther, the passage began to ascend.
It appeared to go upwards, without any end.
The climb was so steep that their muscles grew stiff.
It seemed they were practically scaling a cliff.

Morty, of course, was the first to protest.
“This is awful!” he cried. “What a terrible quest!
Say, look at the map. Are we close to the top?
I’ll tell you, Katrina, I’m ready to flop!”

Katrina, initially, didn’t respond.
She stopped, looking up at the tunnels beyond.
She consulted the map that was guiding the trip,
and lifted a fingertip up to her lip.

“Quiet,” she whispered, “don’t make a sound,
and whatever you do, don’t stumble around.
We’ve almost arrived, but this next little bit—
it’s kind of a doozy, I have to admit.

It's marked on the map like a forest of horns,
like a cluster of bristles and thistles and thorns.
But they'll be up above us, on the roof of the cave.
If we want to get through, then we'll have to be brave.

They're stalactites, you see, that's what they're called.
But these, it would seem, have been badly installed.

It says here they're hung with such delicate poise
that they'll *fall* in response to the tiniest noise!
So be very quiet. Don't hurry or rush.
We're about to go into...

the Tunnel of Hush."

The inside of the passage was muffled and dull.
It was filled with an ancient, luxurious lull,
in which you heard nothing—not even your breath;
for the Tunnel of Hush was as silent as death.

Stepping into the tunnel, they tiptoed ahead.
Morty looked upward with shudders of dread.
Stalactites were hung from the ceiling above,
like the fingers and thumbs of some terrible glove.

Morty was scared. He was looking around,
but up at the ceiling, and not at the ground;
and there, in the dust, just ahead of his boots,
lay a raggedy bramble of creepers and roots.

So Morty, of course, was hardly prepared
when his foot was entangled, his boot was ensnared.
To his credit, mind you, he said nothing at all.
He just fluttered his arms as he started to fall.

He went tumbling, in fact, right smack on his rump,
and the action produced a most audible…

THUMP!

At first, there was nothing, no tumble of rocks,
no plummeting mountain of boulders and blocks.

But then came a noise. Just the tiniest sound:
the

plink

of pebble that fell to the ground.

"Run!"

cried Katrina. "Get up, and let's go!
It's the whole of the roof! It's ready to blow!"

Morty looked up and thought, *What have I done?!*
Katrina was right. The barrage had begun!

Stalactites were falling, like bombs in a war,
skewers of granite and marble and more;
as Katrina and Morty both hurried ahead,
the boulders cascaded wherever they tread.

Like swords, or like sinister sabers of stone,
like jagged and tapering splinters of bone,
they fell to the floor with smashes and bangs,
like a venomous shower of vampire fangs!

"Quick," cried Katrina, "just a little bit more!
It's there, up ahead! The exit! *The door!*"
Each of them saw it, a pocket of light,
a patch of the sky that was blindingly bright;

which now, in their moment of peril and strife,
quite suitably glowed like the promise of life.

Meanwhile, the passage was falling to bits!
A shattering, clattering, battering blitz!

It was then that they made their respective escapes,
but not without bruises and scratches and scrapes.
They dove from the tunnel and onto a hill,
going head over heels, in a dizzying spill.

They rolled down the slope and muddied their pants,
and stopped in a thicket of bushes and plants,
where Morty said, "Well, I guess we've arrived,
and Katrina, guess what? I think we survived!"

Katrina, mind you, was a little bit peeved.
She didn't seem happy, or even relieved.
"Morty, you oaf! You lumbering lout!
We're lucky," she cried, "that we even got out!

You're klutzy! You're clumsy! You're not very deft!
You might have two feet, but they're both of them left!
And speaking of which, it's because of those feet,
that we nearly were mashed into hamburger meat!"

Morty lay still, saying nothing at all.
He remained on his back, laid out in a sprawl.
"I'm sorry," he said, with gasping fatigue,
"This adventuring stuff—it's out of my league."

Katrina just scoffed. She was wondering why,
the zorgles would choose such a blundering guy
to go on a quest, with so much at stake.
To Katrina, it seemed like a dreadful mistake.

Thinking these thoughts, she started to stand.
She took a look round, at the lay of the land.

The view left her breathless, unable to speak.
They were high on the ridge of a mountainous peak,
surrounded by trees of the leafiest green,
in a place where the air was incredibly clean!

Morty stood up. He snuffled the air.
He brushed himself off and he straightened his hair.

And just as he did so, he spotted a sign,
nailed to the trunk of a towering pine.

The branches, however, disguised what it said.
It was partially hidden. It couldn't be read.
Only four of the letters were able to show:

A

Z

and a

G

and an

M

and an

O

But Morty could read it, without any doubt.
In an instant, he easily figured it out.
He turned in a circle. He admired the view.

"WELCOME," he said,

"TO ZORGAMAZOO!"

CHAPTER 8
a *ghost* of a town

When Katrina looked closer and **squinted** her eyes, she was suddenly struck by a hidden surprise...

Concealed in the bushes and blossoming vines,
in the elms and the oaks, in the willows and pines,
behind all the branches, behind all the leaves,
were doorways and windows and shingles and eaves!

"Hellooooo!" Morty hollered, "is anyone here?
Or is it just us…plus the rabbits and deer?"

But no one called back, because no one was there.
The zorgles were gone and the question was: Where?

That, thought Katrina, *is what I'd like to know.*
These countryside zorgles—where would they go?
A whole village of creatures can't fall through the gaps.
They can't just suddenly vanish! Or could they, perhaps?

"Alright," she proposed, "let's knock on some doors!
Let's look in some windows and open some drawers!
It's a mystery, Mort! Like Phillip Marlowe!
Like Sherlock and Watson or Hercule Poirot!"

(Katrina, you see, was a bit of a buff,
when it came to detectives and mystery stuff.)

Morty, of course, he persisted to think
that he was a coward, a phony, a fink,
completely unfit for *mysterious* things
(he was rather more comfortable off in the wings).

But Katrina was right. They should push on ahead.
"Alright then, let's search," he reluctantly said.

"Great," said Katrina. "Now, here's what we'll do:
I think that it's best if we split into two.
We can cover more ground if we do it that way.
It's simply more sensible, wouldn't you say?"

Before Morty could grumble, "Well, *no,* I think not!"
Katrina went rocketing off like a shot.
She was anxious and eager to sniff out the truth,
to play the detective, the snooper, the sleuth.

So Morty, alone, was just a bit scared.
His fingers were trembling. His nostrils were flared.
The whole of his face was a panicky frown,
because Zorgamazoo was a *ghost* of a town.

Meanwhile, Katrina was deep in the wood,
going farther, perhaps, than she probably should.
Yet still, she kept searching and scampering through,
to the outermost fringes of Zorgamazoo.

She came through the trees, before coming to stop
on the rim of a cliff, near a treacherous drop.
She stood there a moment, perched out on the ledge,
on the verge of the mountain's calamitous edge.

The view made Katrina feel suddenly free,
looking over the city, the hills, and the sea.

With her hand, she shielded her eyes from the sun.
It's started, she thought. *My adventure's begun...*

On the edge of the cliff was a towering tree.
It'd grown up as high as Katrina could see,
and surrounding the trunk was a spiraling stair;
so she climbed it, of course, to see what was there.

At the top was a cottage, a cabin of thatch,
built into the trunk, where the branches attach.

The door of the cottage was open a crack.
It creaked in the breeze. It hung eerily slack.
Pushing open the door, Katrina went in,
as a gaggle of goose-pimples prickled her skin.

Inside, the cottage was thoroughly trashed.
The chairs were in splinters, the windows were smashed.
The floor had been scuffed. The dishes were chipped.
Even the pillows and cushions were ripped!

When Katrina saw this, she instantly knew:
These were signs of struggle—and that was a clue!
It meant that the zorgles were *kidnapped*, of course!
They were stolen away! They were taken by force!

Yet this gloomy deduction was only the start.
She knew it was only the tiniest part;
just a droplet of truth in an ocean of doubt,
and soon, other questions were starting to sprout:
questions of *who,* of *why*, and of *how*?
These countryside zorgles—*where* were they now?

As she was thinking and wondering why,
she heard, down below her, *a whimpering cry.*
It rose to a pitch that could bring you to tears
by stirring your soul (or by splitting your ears).

"Who's there?" asked Katrina.
"Who's making that sound?
Hey, Morty, that you? Quit fooling around."

But the wailing went on, like the wind in a squall,
and Katrina could tell: It wasn't Morty at all!
The howling resounded inside of her head,
like a ghostliest, ghastliest wail of the dead.

It was then that she knew it was time to admit:
She and Morty, perhaps—well, they shouldn't have split.
After all, there she was, unaided, alone,
with only this eerie, ethereal moan.

But in spite of her doubts, she valiantly tried
to quell her misgivings, push panic aside,
as she climbed from the tree and down to the ground
to seek out the source of this whimpering sound.

At the bottom, she followed the noise to the edge
of a thicket, an almost impassable hedge.
The branches were dense, so impossibly thick,
that the bramble was virtually made out of brick!

The sound, as she stood there, it started to change,
it sounded less eerie, less fearsome and strange.
Drawing nearer, she realized, it wasn't so bad.
It wasn't so scary, just incredibly…sad.

"Hey," said Katrina, "you sure gave me a scare!
But why're you crying? What's the trouble in there?"

Whatever it was, it let out a *yowl*,
a sob that was more like an animal's growl.

At this point, Katrina assumed that she knew:
This must be a zorgle from Zorgamazoo.
"Hey, listen," she said, "and please, understand:
My friend and I came here to give you a hand."

The creature, however, did nothing but groan.
It let out its loudest, most miserable moan.

"Okay," said Katrina. "I can hear you're upset.
I know I'm a stranger, we've only just met,
but perhaps you can help me. I'm asking you, *please,*
could you do me a favor? Come out of the trees."

But the creature was stubborn. It bellowed some more,
with a moan that was quickly becoming a roar.

"Fine," said Katrina, "just have it your way.
You can whimper and snivel and bellow and bray;
you can splutter and blubber and kick up a din,
but if you don't come out, then I'm coming in."

And so, with a shove and a thrash and a push,
she scraped her way in, through the bramble and bush.
Inside, was a creature. It was curled in a ball.
But it wasn't a zorgle. Oh no, not at all.
It was hardly a zorgle from Zorgamazoo.

No, this thing was

bigger . . .

and *hairier*, too.

CHAPTER 9
a *windigo* beast

The creature, it seemed, was a heaping of curls, its tresses the color of luminous pearls.

"Leave me alone!" cried the mountain of hair.
"You leave me alone…or I'll *eat* you, I swear!
I'll simmer your blood! I'll pickle your legs!
Your eyeballs? I'll fry them like Mexican eggs!"

(Well now. Such violence! Such ominous threats!
Let me tell you, good reader, it gives me the sweats!

Threats such as these, if they ever persist,
they should not be ignored, or simply dismissed.
For example: If someone approached you one day,
some hairy and menacing monster, let's say…

Supposing this monster came over and said:
"Pardon me,
        would you mind if I boiled up your head?"
Well, first you should scream. Then you should run.
Because boiling one's head—well, it isn't much fun.)

So perhaps you'd assume that Katrina Katrell
would run away screaming and yelling, as well.
But no, that was not what our heroine did.
She didn't run off or go flipping her lid.

She stayed where she was. She was perfectly still.
"Sorry," she said, "but I don't think you will."

The creature looked up. There were tears in its eyes,
while under the tears, was a look of surprise.

"Oh no?" said the beast, as it rose to its feet.
"Just come a bit closer. You'll see what I eat!"

The creature stood up, and Katrina could see,
she barely came up to the top of its knee!

This creature was *big*. No, bigger than big,
and covered with hair like a velvety wig.

It had sinewy arms and a generous shape,
resembling some sort of unusual ape.
Its shoulders were sloped. Its knuckles were long.
It might well have come from the Kingdom of Kong.

But what made young Katrina ogle and stare,
were the *ribbons and bows* in the animal's hair!

"You're a girl!" she exclaimed; it came out in a shout.
It was such a surprise, she just blurted it out.

"So what," said the beast, "and what about you?
Maybe you hadn't noticed, but you're a girl, too!
And girlies like you, I usually squish,
because *girl à la mode* is my favorite dish.

You see, my name is Winnie. I'm a windigo beast!
I'm fiercest in all of the west—*and* the east!"

"Okay," said Katrina. "Sure, I understand."
Then she took a step forward and put out her hand.
"Well, my name's Katrina, Katrina Katrell.
It's a pleasure to meet you. Here's wishing you well."

"Bah!" cried the beast. "Get away from me, kid!
You come any closer, you'll regret that you did!"

"C'mon," said Katrina, "you might act like a brute,
but you're not fooling me. See, I'm pretty astute.
You're not really so vicious, not really so bad.
Any nitwit could tell, you're just...kinda sad."

"Oh, reeeeaaally?" said Winnie.
"And should I be impressed?
You think I'm unhappy? You think I'm depressed?!
That I lie around weeping all day and all night?
Well, listen here, missy...You're perfectly right!"

Winnie went back to her bellowing moans,
to her blubbers,
        her whimpers,
                her grumbles, and groans.

"Please," said Katrina, "Just cool it! Calm down!
Your tears are so thick, I could practically drown!
Just take a deep breath and try to relax.
Then tell me what happened. I'm after the facts.

The zorgles who live here—where did they go?
Because I've got a hunch that maybe you know.
Was it some sort of magic, or maybe a curse?
Were they kidnapped by pirates…
                        or burglars…
                                or worse?"

"The zorgles!" wept Winnie. "I remember them well.
"My friends," she said sadly. "Aw, gee, they were swell!
Which is why it's so awful, about the attack.
They were *eaten*, Katrina. They'll never come back!

They ate every zorgle in Zorgamazoo!
They ate everyone up—and my family, too!
They had tentacles! Wings! They had terrible claws!
And they'll eat us up, too, with their slobbery jaws!"

Before Winnie could finish, before she could try,
she stopped...because something went *crackle*, nearby.

"They're back!" Winnie sniveled. "We're done for!
 We're doomed!
We'll be eaten, Katrina! Devoured! Consumed!"

Then came a voice. It was husky and gruff.
"I found you!" It wheezed, with a huff and a puff.

To Winnie, Katrina seemed terribly brave,
as she held up her hand in a casual wave.
Katrina, of course, knew that nothing was wrong.
"Hi, Morty," she said. "What took you so long?"

Morty said nothing. He had stopped where he was,
when he spotted that whimpering tower of fuzz.
"Uh, Katrina?" he whispered. "I think we should go.
That thing's not a zorgle—or didn't you know?"

Katrina just laughed. "Don't be silly," she said.
"There's nothing to fear, nothing to dread.
Morty, meet Winnie. She's a windigo beast.
She's the fiercest in all of the west—*and* the east."
"Uh, hi there," said Morty. He gave her a wave.
(He was trying his best to be stoic and brave).

Winnie looked up. "You're a zorgle," she said.
"But I thought you were eaten! I thought you were dead!"
She came forward, to Morty, like a lumbering rug,
and hoisted him up for a muscular hug.

"Okay!" Morty gasped. "It's true! I'm alive!
But you squeeze any tighter, I doubt I'll survive!"
"You poor thing." Winnie sniffled, "How awful for you.
After all that has happened to Zorgamazoo!"

Then she loosened her grip. She put Morty down
and her face, once again, tumbled into a frown.
She sniffed through her nose. She grimaced, and then,
her eyes started going all teary again.

"Okay!" cried Katrina. "Enough is enough!
I'm sick of this miserable whimpering stuff!"

She was glaring at Winnie, right dead in the eye.
"Just tell us what happened! And try not to cry."

So Winnie was brave. She began to recall,
in every detail, no matter how small,
all that had happened and all that she knew,

of

The Terrible Story of Zorgamazoo...

:(

CHAPTER 10
a terrible tale

In order,
my reader, to finally learn
every **terrible twist**, every **terrible turn**
of Winnie the windigo's **terrible tale,**
you must steady yourself.

Let courage prevail!

Winnie, you see, was rather a mess.
In telling her tale, as maybe you'd guess,
she sniffled a lot—and you should understand,
she was wiping that snot on the back of her hand.

So I'll spare you the boogers, all runny and warm,
and I'll give you her story in summary form:

The windigo usually travel in packs.
They're especially careful to cover their tracks.
They live in the roughest, most mountainous lands,
and scavenge the cliffs, with their family clans.

That's how Winnie was. She was rather the same.
She lived with the clan of her family name,
together in thick and together in thin,
with her uncles and cousins, her kith and her kin.

Winifred Windigo Thistle McPaw,
or "Winnie," of course, as you already saw,
lived on the ridge of a forested peak,
near the banks of a lazy, meandering creek.

The creek overflowed to the valley below,
and perhaps you might guess where the water would go.
It flowed over rocks, with its watery blue,
to a pond in the middle of Zorgamazoo!

So after a morning of hiking around,
traversing the cliffs and the mountainous ground,
the windigo clan would visit their friends,
at the pond where the waterfall finally ends.

You see, countryside zorgles and windigo folk,
go together as well as a laugh and a joke;
and whenever together, in Zorgamazoo,
do you know what the zorgles and windigo do?

Well, let me say this: In all of my days,
and in all of my study of windigo ways,
the fact that I find to be oddest of all
is that windigo love to play Zorgally Ball!

Even Winnie herself (when she wasn't depressed),
was a batter who batted as well as the best;
and that's what she did on the terrible day
when the countryside zorgles were stolen away.

Winnie's own team, the "Growlers" by name,
came down from the cliffs for a sociable game.
When Winnie arrived, she was limber and spry,
with a spring in her step and a gleam in her eye.

She arrived with her Uncle, and Auntie as well,
on a day when the weather was perfectly swell.

The zorgles were waiting. The meadow was groomed;
the uniforms pressed, the equipment perfumed;
the goggles were polished, the bases were buffed,
while up in the bleachers, the cushions were fluffed.
Every helmet was buckled up under a chin,
and at last it was time for the game to begin.

The competition was stiff, the athletics intense.
There were several hits that went over the fence.
One team would score, then the other would lead,
as they flew round the bases with flippery speed...

It was late in the bottom of inning sixteen,
when the crowd had gone silent and oddly serene.
The fate of the game was still up for debate,
and that was when Winnie stepped up to the plate.

On the mound was a zorgle of legend and fame,
so famous you've probably heard of his name.
He was Cyril "The Slinger" Zipzorgle DeYoung,
the finest of flingers that ever had flung.

But Cyril DeYoung wasn't *young* anymore.
He had grey in his hair and his shoulders were sore.
His bones, they were old, they ached with fatigue,
and he no longer played in the Zorgledom League.

Yet still, when he pitched, when he threw,
        when he hurled,
he was still the best flinger in all of the world!

He stood on the mound. He pounded his glove.
For him, this whole game was a labor of love.

He kicked up some dust. He chewed on his lip.
On the zorgally ball, he shifted his grip.

Then he lifted his leg from the place where it stood,
and he slung and he flung just as hard as he could!

The ball soared away…and in one second flat,
Winnie let loose with the crack of her bat!

The ball, like a rocket, went higher than high.
It became just a speck in the blue of the sky.
It went into a cloud that was hanging about.
It went *into* the cloud…but it didn't come out.

Out of the sky, came an ominous *hummm,*
then a clatter as if from the beat of a drum
(but without any rhythm, without any flair,
like the growl of an engine in need of repair).

In an instant, the noise grew incredibly loud,
and it came, so it seemed, from the gathering cloud.
The players looked up. They shielded their eyes.
The cloud was expanding to cover the skies!

Then, all at once, the cloud disappeared,
and there, in the air, when it finally cleared,
humming and hovering up in the breeze,
were *creatures* that buzzed like the bumble of bees.

But bees are so tiny, just wee little shrimps.
These creatures, however, were bigger than blimps!

And each like an octopus fitted with wings,
with tentacles twisting like rubbery strings!
The tip of each tentacle ended in *claws,*
looking anxious to nourish these animals' jaws!

They hung in the air for a second or two,
then dropped from the sky over Zorgamazoo.
They chased after players on both of the teams,
eliciting panic and hideous screams!

The creatures, it seemed, in their terrible way,
thought Zorgamazoo was a dinner buffet!

They would scoop up a zorgle, sometimes even two,
and the windigo players before they were through!
They snapped them all up in their pincers and claws,
and greedily sprinkled them into their jaws!

Even Winnie herself was caught in a claw,
but was thankfully saved by her Auntie McPaw,
who shouted to Winnie, "You give 'em yer all!
Winnie, you *hits* 'em, like ya did with that ball!"

Winnie did just as her Auntie had planned
(she still had that zorgally bat in her hand).

So the moment the beast had her up in the sky,
she prodded the thing in its yellowy eye!

The creature was stunned. It floundered around.
It bobbled with Winnie, who fell to the ground.
She landed with luck in a cushiony bush,
and softened the blow with her cushiony tush.

"Good girl!" cried her Uncle. "Now Winnie, you hear?
You stay in that bush! Stay out of the clear!"

Winnie complied, staying out of the way,
while the others were keeping the creatures at bay.
Yet though they fought back with a spirited fight,
they were hardly a match for the animals' might.

So that was how Winnie had come to survive—
while watching her family swallowed alive!

Having eaten, the creatures leapt up in the sky.
And then Winnie the windigo started to cry…

To Morty, the story was rather inane,
but before he began to protest or complain,
there was one little detail he wanted to check.
"Wait a minute," he said. "Now hold on a sec!

"You mean *Cyril DeYoung?* The best of the best?
If you're playing with him, then I'm pretty impressed.
His flings were like lightening. Aw, man, he could throw!
Used to play for the *Underwood Titans*, you know.

"My Pop used to take me. We'd go to their games.
I knew all of the players, knew all of their names.
But my favorite, of course, was that Cyril DeYoung.
'The greatest of flingers that ever has flung!'"

"You're right," Winnie sniffled, her eyes going damp.
"There's nobody like him. He was truly a champ.
But what does it matter? I mean, Cyril is dead!
He was *eaten*, remember?! It's just like I said!"

"I don't know," Morty said. "It sounds hard to believe.
It's really too horrid to even conceive!
You say flesh-eating monsters? From up in the sky?
I won't be convinced. So don't even try."

Katrina, however, was sure it was true.
She didn't know why, it was simply...she *knew.*
She had only to look into Winifred's eye,
to see it was real, that it wasn't a lie.

"But Morty," she said, "Winnie's being sincere.
She witnessed it all! She was hiding right here.
And now a big part of the mystery's solved,
now that we know there are *monsters* involved!"

"Monsters?" said Morty, with a tremor of doubt
(he hated to think there were *monsters* about).
"Believe me, Katrina, and I have to insist,
creatures like that, they don't really exist."

Winnie sucked in a breath. She held up a hand.
"Mr. Morty," she stammered, "you don't understand—"

Morty ignored her. He was shaking his head.
He folded his arms and dismissively said,
"I've seen all sorts of weirdness, since I was a kid,
but *never* a flying, carnivorous squid!"

Winnie covered her eyes. She grimaced and frowned.
"Uh, Morty," she whimpered, "then *don't turn around.*"
There followed a horrible, ominous *hum*,
and a *clack* like a raspy, mechanical drum.

It was one of the creatures that Morty denied,
and so, as he turned, his eyes going wide,
he realized, too late, that the creatures were *real*,
and that he and his friends…would be their next meal!

And so, before Winnie or Morty could speak,
before even Katrina could utter a shriek,
all three were ensnared in those terrible claws,
and tossed in the creature's

insatiable jaws…

CHAPTER 11
the *moonagerie* crypt

My goodness! It seems that our heroes are **doomed**!

Devoured! Digested! Completely consumed!

It's true. They were eaten (like pickles and pie).
But to call it "The End?" Well, no. That's a lie...

Because Mortimer Yorgle, Katrina Katrell,
who were followed by whimpering Winnie, as well,
they indeed had gone slithering into the maw,
of that ugly monstrosity's slobbery jaw.

They went under its tongue and over its teeth.
They slid down its neck to the belly beneath.
The belly, however, was stiff as a stone,
as if all of its innards were nothing but bone.

"Hold on," said Katrina, "this doesn't make sense.
This stomach has walls like the bars of a fence!
It's all iron and copper and rusty with age.
It's less of a belly, and more of a *cage!*"

"Hmm," Morty wondered, scratching his head.
"What I'd like to know is: Why aren't we dead?"

"You're right!" Winnie cried. "I mean, swallowed alive?!
It's not the sort of a thing you routinely survive."

Before Morty could answer with any reply,
the mysterious creature leapt into the sky;
and wherever the creature was traveling to,
it was far, far away from Zorgamazoo.

There weren't any windows, so there wasn't a view.
They just flew...

and they

f l e w . . .

a n d t h e y f l e w . . . .

and they flew!

The trip wasn't pleasant—it was anything but,
as they thumped in the creature's inflexible gut.

They were shot through the air.
        They were thrown in a flop,
with Winnie the bottom, Katrina the top,
and Mortimer awkwardly crumpled between
(he felt like a steak in a mincing machine).

From their heads to their heels,
        they were queasily tossed,
as if weightlessness won...and gravity lost.

But at last, their momentum began to subside.
It seemed they had come to the end of the ride.

"Phew!" Winnie sighed. "Not a second too quick.
Another minute of that and I would've been sick."

It was then something happened,
        something no one would guess,
an occurrence I frankly find hard to express.
But nevertheless, it happened. It's true.
It was then that the creature...*divided in two.*

It began with a creak in the animal's back,
as the stomach came open by only a crack.

Then little by little, and bit after bit,
the crack opened wide and the innards were lit
with glimmers of eerie, mysterious light,
confirming Katrina's suspicion was right:

Inside of the beast there were pulleys and chains,
where there should have been organs
and muscles
and veins.
Or at least an intestine. Or maybe a spleen.
But no…for the beast was, in fact, a machine!

Our heroes were trapped, like dogs in a pound,
in a cage hanging over the dust of the ground!

"It's a trick!" Morty muttered. "It's some kinda scam!
It's nothing but hokum and flimmery flam!"
A trick? thought Katrina. *That's saying the least.*
But why? Who would build such a hideous beast?

Before she could ponder the matter some more,
on the side of the creature, there opened a door.
It led to a cabin, where a pilot could ride.
But who, thought Katrina, *would travel inside?*
Who could build such a thing, in such odious style?
It must surely be someone incredibly vile!

But the man who came out wasn't wretched at all.
He looked rather normal, though a just a bit small.
There was little, it seemed, that made him stand out.
He wasn't too thin, and he wasn't too stout.

This miniature man was perfectly gray,
while his manner was blank, in a similar way.
His movements were slow, as if studied by rote.
He was lacking in anything worthy of note.

He seemed like a person, whom as soon as you'd met,
you would hardly remember and quickly forget;
a person who sadly is always ignored.
If you glanced at him once, you'd already be bored.

In his hands he was holding a silvery box,
with gauges resembling a series of clocks.
He swiveled a switch with the pad of his thumb
and the creature's machinery started to hum.

The cage was brought down on a hook and a chain,
controlled by a massive, mechanical crane.

Though Katrina was frightened, she tried to be brave.
She could see they were somewhere inside of a cave.
Looking down at the man, feeling helpless and trapped,
she grew very angry and suddenly snapped.

"Excuse me," she said to the miniature man,
"could you answer a question? I'm assuming you can.
There's something, you see, that's a little unclear.
So perhaps you can tell us—

WHY ARE WE HERE?!!!"

The man didn't answer. He was lost in a trance,
as if all he was doing was planned in advance.
He held up the box in his miniature fist.
He toggled the dials with a flick of his wrist.

The crane, with a creak, went winching to work.
It hefted the cage, with a jolt and a jerk.

It lowered them down to the depths of the cave,
like a coffin's descent, to the base of a grave...
The walls were all craggy and chalky with dust,
sallow and furrowed with craters and crust.
They slowly continued their deathly descent,
and things became dimmer, the farther they went.

Then came a light. It was eerie and green.
It threw lingering shadows all over the scene.
And the scene, you may ask? It was bleak! It was black!
There were cages piled up into stack after stack,
in a room like a warehouse, endless with aisles,
with cages and cages that went on for miles!

They were piled all the way to the curve of the roof,
and if things were afoul, then here was the proof:
In every last one was a creature or beast,
there must have been *millions* (or hundreds, at least).

Katrina looked round, with alarm in her eyes.
There were creatures of every conceivable size!

Creatures she'd never encountered before,
CREATURES from stories and legends and lore,
Creatures most people would likely reject.
"They're not real," they would say, or so you'd expect.

But here they all were, looking hopeless and pale,
locked in some sort of a despicable jail.

There were yetis, packed in with the whiskery yecks,
so crowded and cramped, they had cricks in their necks.

In a cage to their left were a satyr and faun;
their shoulders were drooped and their faces were drawn.

Meanwhile, the mermaids were lockedin a pot
(and to tell you the truth, they weren't looking so hot).
There were phoenixes too,
but their feathers were dim,
their fiery eyes had gone dismal and grim.

But surely the worst, the saddest of all,
was a **CREATURE** so broad, so impossibly tall,

that he needed the widest and mightiest cell,
and was fitted with shackles and fetters as well.

He was called the **Behemoth**,
this thundering brute,
this monstrously massive, enormous galoot.
To see him, perhaps, you'd be stricken with dread,
with only a glance at his elephant's head.

But to look at him *here*, in his shackles and chains,
would induce only pity, and sympathy pains.
For in spite of his monstrous, magnificent size,
his trunk was all runny. There were tears in his eyes.

It was curious then that Winnie would smile,
as she peered down the cages, at aisle after aisle.
But smiling she was, as she pointed her claw.
"Look! It's my Auntie and Uncle McPaw!"

So it was true. The windigo clan,
every windigo woman and windigo man,

were locked into cages and huddled in groups,
like curious chickens in miserable coops.

And next to their cages, can you guess who was there?
Creatures with shorter, more whiskery hair. . .
Who were these creatures? I'll bet you know who.
"It's the zorgles," cried Morty, "from Zorgamazoo!
"They're here!" he resounded. "Our adventure is done!
We're finished, Katrina! We found them! We won!"

Katrina was comically rolling her eyes.
"Morty," she said, "a word to the wise:
You *might* be rejoicing a little too soon,
you might want to think about changing your tune.

Just look at the others, they're mostly in tears.
They look like they've been here for hundreds of years!
And what about us? We're not doing too hot.
We've been *kidnapped,* remember? Or have you forgot?
So I hate to sound morbid, or even morose,
but I don't think we're finished—no, not even close!"

"Oh, yeah," Morty frowned, going suddenly glum,
"Well, this is the pits! We should never have come!"

Katrina turned back to the miniature man.
Who was he? she wondered. *What was his plan?*

"Hey, you!" she cried out.

"Do you want some advice?
How 'bout

kidnapping people is not very nice!"

The man remained mute. He said nothing at all.
It was sort of like talking to bricks in a wall.

"You're a lout!" said Katrina. "And a criminal too!
I'd say that you've got some explaining to do!"

But the man only stared. He was cold and aloof.
He twisted his gaze to the curve of the roof.

He flicked yet another electrical switch,
and the whole of the ceiling…it started to *twitch*.
The top of the cave, made of metal and chrome,
opened up and revealed: *a crystalline dome!*

Katrina looked skyward, up through the bars.
She saw that the heavens were littered with stars!
And there, in the distance: their planet, their home!
She could see it—*the Earth*—through the glass
of the dome!

She realized, at once (not a second too soon),
they weren't *there* anymore…
they were up on the moon!

The stranger peered up, looking suddenly meek,
and decided, at last, he was ready to speak.

He spoke as if listlessly reading a script.
"Welcome," he said, "to Moonagerie Crypt.
My name is

Dullbert

Hohummer, the Third,

and you'll be here forever…I give you my word.

So there's no going home. You're all here to stay.
Your planet, like mine, is a loooooong ways away."

He said to Katrina. "But, maybe it's true.
I imagine I've got some explaining to do.
In that case, I'll make it abundantly clear,
as to why you were taken, and why you are here."

So that's what he did.
He plunked down on the ground.
He began to explain, to recount and expound…

CHAPTER 12

graybalon-four

The story of Dulbert Hohummer, the Third

is not like the rest of the story you've heard.

Dullbert had come from a faraway place.

In fact, he belonged to an alien race.

He came from a place called Graybalon-Four,
a planet well-known as a bit of a bore.

It was smaller in size than even the Earth.
It had nothing of Jupiter's generous girth,
and nothing like Saturn's magnificent rings.
It had none of those wondrously singular things.

This was a planet where day after day,
the weather was always the rainiest gray,
and not only the sky, but the sea and the land,
everything gray and stupendously bland.

Why, even the people were grayer than gray,
as if all of their color had faded away.

They had built up their planet with cities and lanes
traveled by Graylian trolleys and trains,
from Graylian houses to Graylian shops,
while traffic was guided by Graylian cops.

Most of them toiled at monotonous jobs,
manufacturing gadgets and thingamabobs.

In the evening, they drove along Graylian roads
to the uniform gray of their boring abodes.

And then, climbing into their Graylian beds,
with Graylian reveries filling their heads,
the Graylian people would finish the day,
with dreams that, of course, were entirely gray.

(Think of counting the granules of sand on a beach,
or imagine a lengthy political speech.
Just think of the utmost deplorable bore.
That's ten times as thrilling as Graybalon-Four!)

But why, you may ask, was it lacking in spice?
Like, wouldn't a *little* excitement be nice?

As with much of this story, the answer is found,
by digging a bit, looking *under* the ground…

Because under the surface of Graybalon-Four,
there was little to look at, even less to explore.
It wasn't like Earth, full of boulders and stones,
and minerals, metals, and dinosaur bones.

Inside of this planet was hollow and bare,
like a ball that was filled with unusual air.

But the air wasn't *air*. It was more of a mist.
It quietly wafted and billowed and hissed.
It would sluggishly swirl. It would languidly teem,
and the name of this vapor was:
Tedium Steam.

It was dreary and almost invisibly pale.
It rolled and it flowed at the pace of a snail.
It curdled and churned in swishes and swarms.
It was *boredom*, you see, in its purest of forms.

Now, before you begin to protest or object,
believe me, good reader, my facts have been checked.

It may strike you as weird, and I know how you feel,
but Tedium Steam, I assure you, *is real*.
It's also on Earth. Yes, we've got it too.
No ifs, ands, or buts! What I'm saying is true!
It's produced as a residue, deep in the brain,
in people whose lives are indelibly plain.
You'll find it near braggarts and prattlers and snobs,

or people with overpaid clerical jobs.
It clouds around people with limited views,
and salesmen with products that no one can use.

It builds up in such people, 'til over the years,
there's so much of the stuff it leaks out of their ears.
And not only from people, but from places as well.
There's a great many places the vapor can dwell.

All around the TV it's especially thick,
which is why a TV can make some people sick.
It can also be found in the emptiest nooks
of bookshelves that no longer have any books.

While this Tedium Steam, for whatever it's worth,
is not really noticed, down here, on the Earth,
up on Graybalon-Four, the stuff is like gold!
It was mined from the ground. It was traded and sold.

In fact, it was used as an energy source,
to power their trains (and their buses, of course).
All that Tedium Steam, through the night and the day
kept everything moving in every which way.

There were steam-powered toasters
    and steam-powered drills.
There were steam-powered factories,
    steam-powered mills.
There were steam-powered houses
    and steam-powered cars,
and steam-powered everything under the stars!

And so, over time, it would certainly seem,
that Graybalon-Four…would run out of Steam.

The politicians, you see, had stiffly decreed:
"There's a ton of the stuff! Even more than we need!
There's more," they declared, "than at first it appears!
There's enough to last upwards of billions of years!"

So all of the people on Graybalon-Four,
built factories, houses and buses galore!
Because everyone thought, without even a doubt,
that their Tedium Steam—it would never run out.

Politicians, however, are commonly wrong,
and the Tedium Steam didn't last very long.

Where once the whole planet had "more than enough,"
there soon was a worrying lack of the stuff.

So the Graylians gathered on Parliament Hill.
Some were shaking their fists.
        Some were solemn and still.

"Prime Minister, sir!" the Graylians cried.
"You said we had tons! But we haven't! *You lied!"*

Unmoved, the Prime Minister uttered a snort.
In his mind, he was planning a pithy retort.
But before he could speak, he was rather amazed
to hear someone's voice being suddenly raised.

"Wait!" said the voice. "Please! Hold on a sec!
Our situation is grim! It's a bit of a wreck!
But here's what I'm thinking: If we've got the guts,
then I've an idea—and it might save our butts."

The Prime Minister, startled, looked over the crowd.
He adjusted his glasses and shouted aloud,
"Who said that? Who are you? Which one of you spoke?
I certainly hope you weren't making a joke!"

(You see, telling a joke or pulling a prank,
on Graybalon-Four, was like robbing a bank.
If you said to a stranger, *"Knock, knock,"* or *"Who's there?"*
you'd be dragged off to jail by the roots of your hair.)

"Oh no," said the voice, sounding suddenly small,
"It wasn't a joke! No-no, not at all!
I was telling the truth. I've thought of a way,

to keep everything
working and
perfectly gray."

The Prime Minister paused. He squinted. He stared.
(He was old, after all, and his sight was impaired.)
"Well, whoever you are, before making your claim,
you first must come out! You must tell us your name!"

The crowd moved aside. It was parted in two,
and the stranger came forward.
He pushed himself through.

He stood on his toes, to better be heard.
"I'm

Dullbert," he said,

"Hohummer, the Third. . ."

CHAPTER 13
an *insidious* plan

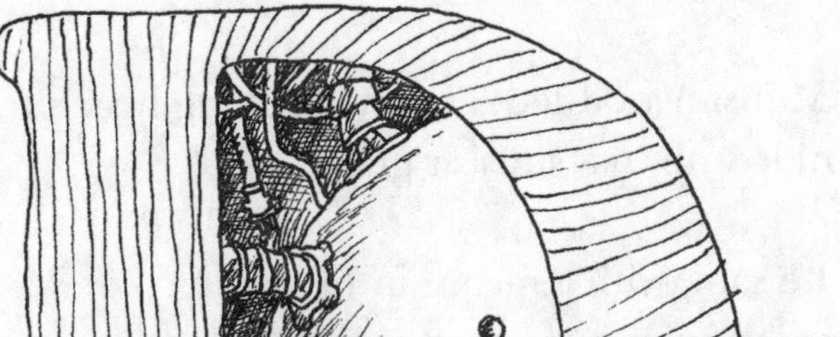

ullbert,

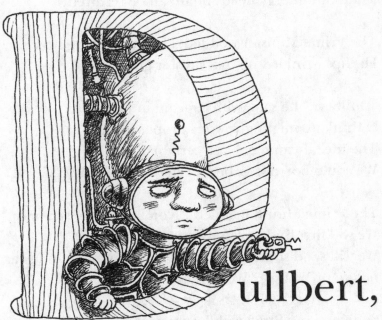

hello," the Prime Minster said,

"so what's this idea that you've got in your head?"

"Well, now," said Dullbert, "here's what I thought:
Maybe Tedium Steam can be borrowed or bought.

We could trade with some place
        where the people are bored.
Then our energy needs might all be restored!"

The Prime Minister nodded. He was stroking his chin.
His lips wrinkled up in a sinister grin.

"Dullbert," he said, with a gleam in his eye,
"I think we might give your proposal a try.
The idea, I can see, has a certain appeal.
We could borrow, or beg, or maybe—*just steal.*"

The Prime Minister smiled. "Now, here is *my* scheme:
We will first find a planet with Tedium Steam.
We will send someone there, with equipment and gear,
to steal it! You see? We have nothing to fear!"

So telescopes fitted with lenses of glass,
were built to seek out this intangible gas.
They incessantly gazed at the gray of the skies,
with the glint of their massive, monocular eyes.

They scanned every comet and planet and sun,
Every orb in the sky—every single last one!

Every nebula, galaxy, near and afar,
every planet and moon, every wandering star,
every current of ether and heavenly gust,
and every last speckle of meteor dust!

For years, all the Graylians peered at the sky,
in search of a surrogate power supply;
and after so long, they were set to collapse.
They were ready to quit, to throw in their caps.

They were fully convinced that their planet was doomed.
We're done for, they thought. (Or so they assumed.)

It was Dullbert, at last, who found a surprise:
a greeny-blue planet of limited size.
What he found in this place, it would certainly seem,
was the tiniest whisper of Tedium Steam!

"Kalloo and kallay," the Prime Minister said,
giving Dullbert a pat on the top of his head.
"Let's have a look closer. How much have they got?
Because Dullbert," he muttered, "we need quite a lot."
But the problem was this: There wasn't enough.
There was barely a trace, just a puff of the stuff.

You see, these were the days (and the evenings) of yore,
when the Earth was exciting and less of a bore.
Back then it was brimming with creatures and things,
like dragons and ogres and griffins with wings.

Our planet, back then, was a wondrous affair,
and boredom itself was exceedingly rare!

The Prime Minister frowned. He threw up his hands.
"Curses!" he cried. "They're foiling our plans!
Just look at it, Dullbert! Of course that's the case.
It's lively, exciting! *Blegh*—what a terrible place!"

The Prime Minister paused. "Wait a moment," he said.
"What if this place were a little more...dead?

"If the planet were drabber, I think we would find
that the people, as well, would be rather inclined
to get splendidly sick with the drearies and dulls,
so that Tedium Steam would come out of their skulls!
But how can we keep them all jaded and bored,
so our energy needs can be fully restored?"

"Well, now," said Dullbert, "between you and me?
It's all of those **CREATURES**.
They're the problem, you see.
They live in the rivers, the woodlands and peaks,
these astonishing BEASTIES and lovable **freaks**!

So whenever those 'humans' go out for a stroll,
they encounter a yeti, a gorgon, a troll,
which makes them all bubbly with wonder and awe,
and enchanted, you see, from whatever they saw.

This enchantment, it lingers,
bit like a dream,
and it blocks their production of Tedium Steam.
So what if those creatures were taken away?
This Earth would be duller, now wouldn't you say?"

The Prime Minster blinked. He nodded his head.
"Dullbert, you're brilliant!" he finally said.
"We'll start off with all the most fanciful ones.
This planet, regretfully, has them in tons!

Creatures with features so eerily weird,
it would surely be *best* if they all…disappeared.

Once they're all gone, our plan will succeed!
We'll have Tedium Steam—
we'll have all that we need,
once this planet is colorless, boring, bereft…
once there aren't any creatures or animals left!

We'll **KIDNAP** them all! We'll pilfer and steal,
'til humans forget that they *even are real!"*

So together, the Graylian people began
to contrive and devise an insidious plan.

Kidnapping robots were hastily made
to pirate and pilfer, to pillage and raid;
and these robots, these monsters, these *Octomabots,*
they were only the start of the sinister plots…

The following phase of the devious scheme
was something to gather up Tedium Steam.

They called it a *Hoarder of Boredom Machine.*
It would search any place with a weary routine.
It would seek out the Steam, and no matter where,
it would siphon the boredom right out of the air.
It would vacuum it up, from the Earth to the moon,
inflating its core like a massive balloon.

The contraptions were packaged and carefully stored.
They were taken to rockets and loaded aboard.

Then came the time for selecting the one
who would finish the job that now had begun:
a Graylian hero to lead the attack,
who would travel to Earth...and might never come back.

So the Graylian people were put to a vote.
Each of them wrote on a balloting note;
and the one they selected, the one they preferred,
was none other than Dullbert Hohummer, the Third.

Upon hearing the news of the Graylian's choice,
Dullbert wasn't upset, though he didn't rejoice.

He merely stood calmly, somber, and still.
"I'll do it," he said. "Yes, I imagine I will."

He climbed into one of those Octomabots,
and although he was nauseous, his stomach in knots,
he said not a word, just uttered a sigh,
as he watched all the Graylians, waving goodbye.

Then the countdown began. It went backward from ten.
The rockets ignited, they rumbled, and then:
blew cindering billows all over the place,
as Dullbert Hohummer was launched into

spac e . . .

CHAPTER 14
the *hero* himself

When Dullbert arrived

at the end of his tale,
he seemed hollow and breathless, pallid and pale.
His eyes, they were fixed on the dark of the night.
"I'm sorry," he said. Then he switched off the light.

"Come back!" called Katrina. She clutched at her bars.
She rattled her cage, by the light of the stars.
But there was no answer, just silence and gloom,
as phantomlike shadows rose up in the room.

"We're done for,"

said Winnie, who started to cry.
"We'll languish in here 'til the day that we die!"

Morty, meanwhile, uttered nothing at all.
He was hunched in the corner, curled up in a ball.

He was trying his utmost to whistle a tune,
to cheer himself up, with his usual croon.
But all of his music was caught in his throat,
so that nothing came out, not one single note.

"I say!" said a voice. "Yes, haven't we met?
I'm certain we have. I would never forget!"
It came from a creature, half-eagle, half-cat,
in a cage near the one in which Mortimer sat.

This was a griffin—part-lion, part-bird.
He grinned in his cage. He chirped. Then he purred.
He was staring at Morty with wonder and awe.
And for whatever reason, he liked what he saw.

"You've come!" he exclaimed. "I knew it was you!
And take it from me—you're *way* overdue.
But one thing's for sure, you look pretty good,
younger, I'd say, than I figured you would.
A bit chubby, perhaps, but perfectly fit.
You hardly have changed, not even a bit!"

It took Morty a moment to figure it out:
that *he* was the one being spoken about.
"I'm sorry," he said. He was rather bemused.
"I don't think we've met. You must be confused."

"No-no," said the griffin, "you misunderstand!
I know that old face like the back of my hand!"
He called to the others. He summoned the troops.
They gawked from their cages in curious groups.

"Over here!" called the griffin. "Look who it is!
It's that valiant explorer! That wandering whiz!
They told us this guy was incurably sick,
but that was just drivel, just some sort of trick!

"Because here he is now, no longer at large!
He'll help us escape! He'll be leading the charge!
I know you all know him, from ogre to elf:
It's **Bortlebee Yorgle**,
the hero himself!"

The words of the griffin were taken as cause
for whooping and cheering and joyous applause!

Morty, however, was sort of ashamed.
It wasn't his fault; he couldn't be blamed.
"Folks. . ." he said quietly, shifting his weight.
"I'm sorry to have to set all of you straight.

I wish I could help. I mean, we're in a jam!
But I'm not the zorgle you think that I am.
So my news isn't good, but rather it's bad.
You've got me mixed up, I think, with my dad."

The griffin stepped backward, clicking his tongue.
"I suppose that your right. You're just a bit young.

But wait!" he went on, that magical beast.
"You're a *Yorgle*, remember? That's something, at least.
That's a name we admire, a name we revere.
It means something special to everyone here!"

The others agreed. They knew Bortlebee well.
And all of them there had a story to tell…

The **mermaids**, for instance,
recounted a time,
when Bortlebee Yorgle was still in his prime,
exploring the sea that lay under the waves,
the channels and currents, the coral and caves;
in a green submarine, through bubble and brine,
to depths where the water was darker than wine.

It was there he discovered a mystical town,
glowing like jewels in the crest of a crown:

a silver metropolis, gleaming and sleek.
But the town called "Atlantis" was springing a leak!

So he made the repairs, with the help of his sub,
like plugging the drain when you hop in the tub.
And for saving their home in the briny abyss,
the mermaids gave Bortlebee Yorgle... *a kiss!*

A pixie named Qwixi was next to recall
how her people had learned to play Zorgally Ball.

She spoke of her youth, on the Malabar coast,
where the sand was as pale as the soul of a ghost;
where life was idyllic, untroubled and free,
on the fanciful banks of the Indian sea.

One evening, a zorgle was found on the shore.
He was dripping and drowning and soaked to the core.
Unconscious, he lay like a heap in the sand,
with an odd looking sphere in the palm of his hand.

Little-by-little, the zorgle revived,
bewildered and grateful at having survived.

Since his manner was one that the pixies could trust,
they mended his wounds with their magical dust.

He explained how a storm had demolished his boat,
despite all his efforts to keep it afloat;
and how, when his vessel was lost in the squall,
the one thing he could save…was his zorgally ball.
The pixies were puzzled. It seemed a bit daft.
Why not a compass, a paddle, *a raft?!*

When they'd asked him this question, Bortlebee sighed.
I'll just have to show you, he swiftly replied.
So that's what he did: He showed them the way.
And they *still* play the game…to this very day!

Then a **dragon** named Eddie,
enfeebled and old,
recalled how he once had lost all of his gold…

He had just sold his lair and moved to a grot,
but discovered his home was unbearably hot.
(The cave, after all, had never been toured
by the *Dragonish Real-Estate Marketing Board!)*

So Eddie, of course, had a terrible shock
when his home bubbled over with lava and rock!

But lucky for him, he escaped by a hair
by flapping away in the smoldering air.

His treasure, however, was lost in the blast,
as Eddie stood watching, agape and aghast.
His grot went **KABOOM** and his treasure was hurled
to every lost corner in all of the world!

Yet though Eddie's treasure could hardly be saved,
on every last penny, his name was engraved.
So as long as the pieces weren't melted or burned,
he hoped that someday it might all be returned.
Then one day, it was. A package arrived.
It was proof that some part of his treasure survived!

And then there were more, coming one every day,
from places obscure and out of the way.
Packages brimming with shiny doubloons
or glimmering goblets and runcible spoons;
and each with a letter, signed off at the end:

Sincerely,
B. Yorgle,
your wandering friend!

The **creatures** recounted.
They all reminisced.
They couldn't hold back. They couldn't resist.
They each had astonishing tales to relate,
old Bortlebee legends of danger and fate!

And then, in the end, when at last they were done,
having laughed, having wept, have shared in the fun,
they all turned to Morty, their eyes full of trust,
and said to him,

"Please! You can save us! *You must!*"

Morty just shrugged. "Well, what can I do?
I'm even more hapless and hopeless than you."

As the words left his lips, you could see all around how the faces had fallen, how everyone frowned. It seemed all the hope had been sucked from the moon,

like the air going out of a punctured balloon.

It was then that their captor came sauntering back,
his languid expression predictably slack.

"Good morning," said Dullbert Hohummer, the Third.
He was followed by robots, who wobbled and whirred.
They were dressed in tuxedos and carrying trays,
like waiters in lavishly fancy cafés.

They bustled about, like bees all abuzz,
and Katrina was struck by how hungry she was.
Her stomach was rumbling. She moistened her lips.
She was dreaming of succulent nibbles and sips!
She was ready to gobble, to guzzle, to scarf,
but seeing the food...she was ready to barf!

"Eeewwww!" she exclaimed, her blood running cold.
"It looks like manure that started to mold!"

"You're right," said a yeti, who grumbled and sighed.
"The first time I ate it, I practically died!
But that's all we get. It's all that we're fed—
the grayest of gruel and the stalest of bread."

And so they were served this slippery slop,
plopped into bowls with a *glup* and *glop*,
It was slimy and lumpy and thoroughly rank.
And the way that it *reeked!* Believe me—it stank!

Dullbert stood back, surveying the scene.
He blinked as the creatures went queasy and green.

"You know," he said absently, tilting his head.
"I was snooping before, and I heard what you said.
This 'Bortlebee Yorgle,' this one you respect?
He's among the next victims I'm set to collect.

Oh, I'll try to be delicate. I won't be too rough.
But I'm on my way now to Underwood Bluff.
The zorgles who live there are last on my list.
It's important, you see, that no one is missed."

"You can't!" Morty cried. "My father's too old!
He's sick! And he can't even handle the cold!
He shouldn't be moved. He's feeble and frail!
His heart is so weak, it'll probably fail!"

"I'm sorry," said Dullbert. "Just doing my job."
He took out his watch, which hung on a fob.
"I've no time to chat. I have to prepare.
This business, you see, is a tricky affair.
And sadly I see that I'm falling behind.
So I'll be on my way, if none of you mind."

He bid them goodbye with a spiritless wave,
and left, through the shadowy door of the cave.

Morty said nothing, just stood there and stared.
He was rigid with rage, but he also was scared.
He began to feel faint. He began seeing spots,
recalling with terror those Octomabots.

"Katrina," he said, his mouth going dry.
"I'm feeling like Winnie. I'm ready to cry."
He slid down his bars to the mesh of the floor,
feeling even more gloomy than ever before.

Katrina went over to offer some cheer,
to say something kind into Mortimer's ear.
But what could she say? What could she do
for a friend who felt so inconsolably blue?

So gently, she rested her hand on his head.
Because sometimes our words…

. . . are best left unsaid.

CHAPTER 15

a *wing* and a prayer

It was then something *rather surprising* occurred.

A *noise* drifted up, like the chirp of a bird;
like a floor, giving way with the tiniest creak,
it was reedy and shrill, going:

squim - squibble - squeak!

In the cage just below her, an ogre was there.
He was polishing something, with hanks of his hair.
The object was round, like a peach or a plum,
which the ogre had clenched in his finger and thumb.

He would spit on the object, then polish and rub,
giving every last inch a meticulous scrub.
Therein lay the source of the curious sound,
as he burnished this *thing* that was perfectly round.

The **ogre**
himself was the
usual kind.
He was crooked, decrepit and hardly refined.
Though his arms and his legs
    were spindly and svelte,
his belly was plump. It hung over his belt.

His jowls were like rubber, his nose like a twig.
His feet were all grubby and terribly big.
He was old in his bones and he needed a shave.
He already, it seemed, had one foot in the grave.

Katrina, intrigued, put her face to the floor.
She had never encountered an ogre before.
"Excuse me," she said. "Hello there. I'm new.
I've only just come to this weird little zoo."

The ogre looked up, his face like a mutt.
His one eye was open. The other one shut.
"Well, missy," he said, with a yellowy smile,
"you'll be here forever! Or at least for a while."

He laughed at his joke, with a rascally smirk,
going back to the *squeaks* of his polishing work.

Katrina, still curious, wanted to know
what it was that he did in his prison below.

"Sir?" she inquired, acting prim and polite,
"May I ask you a question, to see if I'm right?
That bauble you're shining, like silver or brass,
I'll bet it's your *eyeball.* Is it made out of glass?"

"It is," said the ogre. "It's a pretty good fake.
I take care of it, see? So it won't ever break."
Then he held it aloft, with the pupil in view.
"So, yes, it's my eyeball—and what's it to you?!"

"Well," said Katrina, "here's what I think:
We can get ourselves free of this miserable clink!
Because I've an idea that I'm willing to try,
but the key to my plan, good sir...is your eye."

The ogre recoiled. He cowered and flinched.
His eyeball, he clutched and he clenched
    and he clinched;

he squelched it back into its usual place,
in the wrinkly and puckered-up hole in his face.

Then he paused for a moment.
He looked up and he smiled.
He regarded Katrina with eyes like a child.
"Escape?" he said vaguely. "You think that we can?
In that case, okay then. Let's try with your plan."

He plucked out the eye from the hole in his head,
"Be careful, it's precious," he breathlessly said.
Then, with a gesture like motherly love,
he held up his eye, to the shadows above.

Katrina, up top, lay flat on her side.
She reached through the bars, her hand open wide.

After they made this uncommon exchange
(the swap of an eye; it was certainly strange!),
the ogre's long arms fell limp at his hips.
He looked to Katrina with quivering lips.

A tear trickled out from his one seeing eye.
This cantankerous ogre…he had started to cry.

"Don't fret," said Katrina. "There's really no need,
if we follow my plan, I think we'll be freed.
Dullbert, you see, he's forgotten that box,
the one that controls all the cages and locks."

It was true: There it was, on a shelf by the door,
a long way away—fifty meters, or more.
It sat there, just blinking, that special remote,
like a faraway lighthouse that beckons a boat.

"There it is," said Katrina, "on a shelf, over there.
If we smash it, I think, beyond any repair,
then the locks will malfunction, they'll go on the blink,
and we'll stage an escape…at least, that's what I think.

So my plan is to smash it by throwing your eye.
We've got little to lose. So I'll give it a try."
As the ogre stood cringing and wincing below,
Katrina wound up. She got ready to throw.

"Stop!" came a cry, from near where she stood.
"It's too far! You can't do it! Almost nobody could!"

It was Morty. He was suddenly back on his feet.
"To throw it that far, you need serious heat!"

Then Winnie piped up, her eyes going wide.
"There is only *one person* to do it!" she cried.

Morty looked at Katrina, surprisingly calm.
"That's right," he agreed, and he put out his palm.
"If you need something thrown,
        something flawlessly flung,
you need Cyril "the Slinger" Zipzorgle DeYoung."

Katrina just smiled, with a grin like a cat.
"Of course," she replied. "I knew you'd say that."
She handed the eyeball to Morty, and then,
it was handed to others, again and again.

It was passed through the bars from finger to claw,
from dragon to pixie, from talon to paw.
Until, at long last, the eyeball arrived
(a bit sullied, perhaps, but having survived),
in the place
        where the zorgles were huddled and cramped,
trapped in a cage that was bolted and clamped.

Although they were crowded, for that was the case,
they managed to shuffle and clear out a space.
And there, in their midst, looking timid and shy,
was Cyril DeYoung. . .
        and they passed him the eye.

Katrina said: "Cyril, it's just like a ball,
and we need you to throw it. Just fling it, that's all.
But whatever you do, give it all that you've got.
It has to be perfect. We've got only one shot."

Cyril looked at the eye. He hefted its weight.
He could throw it, he thought, and perfectly straight;
but he'd never, however, thrown ever so far,
or thrown with a ball so extremely bizarre.

"I don't know," Cyril said. "The truth being told,
that's a pretty long way. . . and I'm getting old.
I used to throw hard, I used to throw fast,
but my arm's not as strong as it was in the past.

A few years ago now, perhaps five, maybe ten.
I might've been able to throw it—back then.

But the problem is, folks, that's one heck of a lob.
It's too far for me. I'm too old for the job."

Morty went to his bars. He said, "Mr. DeYoung!
Don't forget! You're the finest who ever has flung!
I remember you playing, back when I was a tyke.
All those pitches you made—I mean, *strike* after *strike!*
Well, anyway, sir, I'm your number-one fan,
and I *know* you can do it, or else. . . nobody can."

Cyril looked at the eyeball, at its singular stare.
It looked back at him, hopeful—like everyone there.
He knew then he'd try. There was no other choice.
"I'll do it," he said, in a whispering voice.

He started to stretch, started limbering up.
He flapped both his arms with a *whip* and a *whup.*
He narrowed his eyes. He chewed on his lip.
The eyeball, he squeezed, and he shifted his grip.

He lifted his leg from the place where it stood.
Then he flung that old eyeball as hard as he could.

It went off like a streak, like a shot from a gun.
It zipped through the bars, without touching a one.
It careened as it flew. It spun through the air.
It was off on its own, on a wing and a prayer.

Then it started to fall, began losing its steam.
Too early, perhaps! Or so it would seem.
But then, at the end of its elegant arc,
Everyone knew: It was right on the mark!

As Katrina had planned, right from the start:
It **WHACKED** it! It **CRACKED** it! It blew it apart!
It ended its flight like a thunderous punch.
It shattered the box, with a rupturing **CRUNCH**!

But sadly, the ogre, through the bars of his cell,
could see that his eyeball had shattered as well.

"My eyeball!" he cried. "Oh, what'll I do?!"
He glared at Katrina. "It's your fault! It's you!
I'll look like a pirate! I'll be wearing a patch!
I might as well find me a parrot to match!"

He threw up his hands. He spat on the floor.
He angrily kicked at the steel of his door.

And just as he did, as he kicked from inside,
The door gave a creak...then it opened up wide!

"Huh," said the ogre. "Well, that's a surprise.
Who cares if I've only got one of my eyes,
because look! It's almost too good to be true!
We're freeeeeeee, Miss Katrina! It's all thanks to you!"

The ogre was right. They were coming undone:
every cage, every lock, every single last one.
Each manacle, bridle, every linkage of chain—
they all opened up, as if sharing a brain.

All these creatures that people believed were extinct,
they all stood in shock. They muttered and blinked;
and then, one by one, they opened their doors,
coming forward like veterans of too many wars.

Winnie looked over, and guess who she saw?
Her cousins, with Uncle and Auntie McPaw!

"We're free," said her uncle,
        "thanks to you and your friend!
Our troubles, perhaps, they've come to an end!"

"Maybe," said Morty. "Don't get hopeful too soon.
Remember, McPaw, we're still stuck on the moon."

What Morty was saying was certainly true,
and the facts of the matter were worse than he knew...
Along all the walls and just out of sight,
mysterious figures were coming to light.
At first, no one noticed and nobody saw:
the flicker of wings...and of teeth...and of claw.

The Octomabots were coming their way,
like lions and tigers, approaching their prey,
with pincers and grabbers all ready to snap,
preparing a perfectly treacherous trap.

But neither Katrina, nor Morty to boot,
had a sense of their nasty pursuer's pursuit.

From left and from right came a shadowy shape.
So the question, good reader, is:

Could they escape?

CHAPTER 16
a *furious* fray

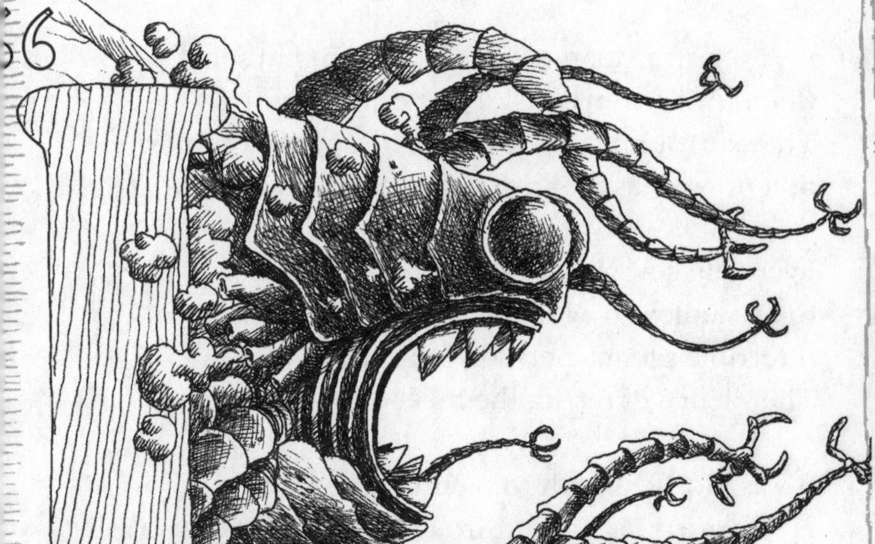

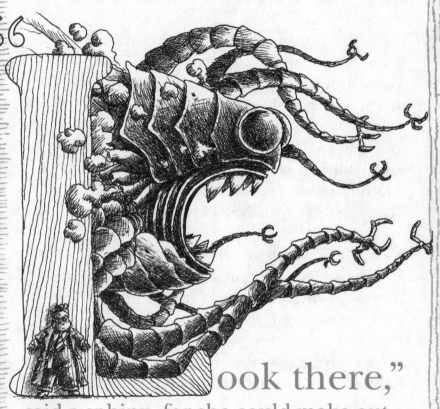

"Look there,"
said a sphinx, for she could make out—
the darkness nearby…it was moving about.
At first only shadows. Then suddenly: **CLAWS!**
Then bellies and wings and finally: **JAWS!**

"They're back!" Winnie blubbered. "I guess this is it!
You'll excuse me, of course, if I whimper a bit."

It was hard to blame Winnie for being upset,
when the Octomabots were closing their net.
They surrounded their prey like a poisonous moat,
or a noose—as it narrows and strangles a throat.

Everyone cowered, resigned to their fate:
to be swallowed again, like some fisherman's bait.
A terrible silence pervaded the air:
The silence of terror, the hush of despair.

It was Morty himself who ended the hush.
He wormed his way in through the huddle and crush.
He was thinking, you see, of Katrina Katrell.
If she could be brave, maybe he could, as well.

He came to the core of that cowering crowd.
He stood on his tip-toes, he shouted aloud:

"Now, sometimes you lose and sometimes you win,
but my Pop always told me:

You *never* give in!

And if he were here now, I know what he'd say:
Morty, my son, when you're caught in a fray,
or your travels are tough and the going is rough,
or you're up to your neck in the slippery stuff,
or say some old robots are on the attack,
then I tell you, my son: **You start fighting back!'**

Hearing this improvised rallying cry,
the creatures of Earth decided to try.
They'd work all together. They'd give it their all,
like a team on the field, playing Zorgally Ball.

They stood, all together, in steely suspense.
Their eyes were unblinking. Their muscles were tense.

Morty looked round, with an arch of his brow.
"That's it," he said softly, "just wait for it now.
Just wait...and we'll take them, I think, by surprise.
Just wait...'til you make out the whites of their eyes."

But the Octomabots, they were smarter than that,
and one of them lunged, right off the bat.
It moved blindingly quick, but be that as it may,
the Behemoth was there, and he stepped in its way.

He snatched up its tentacles—six in a fist!—
and he hefted it up with a heave and a twist,
so the Octomabot, its whole body and all,
went sailing away and smashed on the wall!

The Behemoth was stunned. He was rather impressed.
"I don't know my own strength!" he sincerely confessed.

"All right," Morty cried, "let's give 'em what for!
That was only the first. There's a great many more!
But if we stick together, like paper and glue,
then I think we can take them, I honestly do!"

And so, all at once, a great battle began
(you might say the hooey was hitting the fan).
The battle went crashing all over the place,
between creatures of Earth,
and the creatures from space!

The giants *galumphed* with a

BIFF!

and a

BOFF!

While the punches of pixies went

piffle!

and

poff!

The griffins, whose wings had been formerly pinned,
soared up in the air, like hawks in the wind.
They snatched up the arms of the Octomabots,
and, looping in circles, they tied them in knots!

Even the tiniest creatures of all,
the faeries and imps (who were awfully small),
they, too, waded into the furious fray,
and were helping to fight, in their miniature way.

On the robots they leapt, with the greatest of care,
going deep underneath all the layers of hair.
They went under the arms, where they tickled the pits,
so the robots were reeling in snickering fits!

Soon the Octomabots were battered and bruised,
looking messy, disheveled, and rather confused.
But still they fought on. They were stubborn and stout.
They continued to bully their muscles about,
thrashing and flailing their pincers and claws,
gnashing and grinding their slavering jaws.

So the battle raged on for the Octomabots,
against dragons and manticores, covered with spots;
against sphinxes and griffins and ogres and elves,
all struggling together, defending themselves!

It was then that Katrina was struck with a thought,
of a way they could maybe avoid being caught.
"Morty!" she bellowed. "You stay here and fight!
I'm going off now, to set everything right!"

"But how?" Morty wondered. "I don't understand.
And where are you going? What've you planned?"

But Katrina had vanished, without leaving a trace.
In the spot where she'd been, there was nothing but

space.

Not again, Morty thought, as he muttered a sigh,
while dodging a tentacle, slithering by.
Katrina was smart, that much was true,
but honestly, what could she possibly do?

There was only one person who saw where she went.
He was stooping and crooked and thoroughly bent;
and this aging, decrepit, cantankerous guy
had ironically seen her with only *one eye*.

Watching her vanish, having heard what she said,
he winked, with that vacuous hole in his head.
"Good luck," said the ogre, with a weak little wave,
"You're probably nuts...but you're certainly brave!"

CHAPTER 17

inside the *machine*

imagine, of course,
you're eager to know: Where was Katrina?

Where did she go?

You're wondering where and you're wondering how.
Wait six little words...

and

I'll

tell

you

right

now:

Looking behind her, Katrina had seen,
a hatch in the Hoarder of Boredom Machine.
She opened it up with the tip of her shoe,
and clambered inside, then vanished from view.

Down through a passage, she quietly sneaked,
while in every direction, machinery creaked.

The farther she went, the passages shrank,
the workings grew cluttered and dingy and dank,
but still she pressed on, going all in between
the wires and tubes making up the machine.

She finally came to the end of the road,
to a nexus, where all the machinery flowed.
There, she encountered a mountainous sphere:
An incredible orb that was perfectly clear.

It rose from the floor like a planet of glass.
It was filled with an *almost invisible gas.*
The gas had the color of moldering cream,
and Katrina knew then: this was Tedium Steam!

She took a step forward, approaching the sphere.
It loomed overhead, looking bleak and austere.

She spotted two wires, two cables, two cords,
that sprung from the floor and went curling towards
the base of the sphere and its silvery glass,
where they linked to the bottom, with fittings
of brass.

Seeing them there, something clicked in her mind
as she looked at the way the machine was designed.
Those wires, she thought. *They are the way
of solving our problems and saving the day!*

She took off her bag, slipping out of the straps.
She opened it slowly, unzipping the flaps.
Inside was a clutter, a jumbled array,
of all she'd collected since running away:

The spring that had come from a grandfather clock,
the one she had used to jimmy the lock…

Some strips of the sheet that had flapped like a cape,
when she'd leapt from her window to make her escape…

There was also a knife she had grabbed in a flash,
from the hair of that bully, Selena the Slash…

There were pebbles and stones,
          from the Tunnel of Hush,
she had caught when they fell
          in that plummeting crush…

She had even acquired some slippery slime,
the oiliest, goopiest, greasiest grime.
It had come from the tongue of the Octomabot,
and clung to her bag like a dollop of snot.

Using the knife from Selena the Slash,
she proceeded to sever, to mangle, and gash.

Then with the pebbles and some of the rocks,
she scraped and she hammered
with scratches and knocks.

The spring—it was twisted and given a flip,
so its coil became more of a fastening clip.

With all of these items, she fiddled around,
using all of the various things she had found.

At last, when her curious work was complete,
she tied it all off with the tatters of sheet,
and sealed it like glue with the gunk that had hung
from the Graylian robot's mechanical tongue.

Then she stood back, her eyes going wide.
Something *peculiar* was starting inside...

At the heart of that shimmering, luminous sphere,
a *new* kind of vapor began to appear.

It started quite slow. At first, just a puff,
from one of the tubes that was pumping the stuff.
A new kind of gas was replacing the old,
and the new stuff, in truth, was a sight to behold!

Inside of the glass, to Katrina's surprise,
was a music, it seemed,

you could hear
with your eyes...

Meanwhile, outside of the Boredom Machine,
the battle was growing ferocious and mean.

The creatures of Earth, the zorgles and all,
were locked in a brazen and barbarous brawl:
There was hair being wrangled, eyes being poked,
toes being twisted and throats being choked!
Morty and Winnie were taking their lumps!
The sphinxes and griffins were covered with bumps!
The dragons, the yetis, the phoenixes too,

the pixies and fauns and the Gillygaloo,
were lost in fracas of wallops and bonks,
of punches and pummels and clobbers and clonks!

But in spite of their vow that they never would quit,
in spite of their bravery, gumption and grit,
they were starting to tire, losing their hopes,
like a boxer, pinned down, his back on the ropes.

The Octomabots, they too could surmise,
with the ominous gleam in their ominous eyes
that the battle was finally taking its toll,
and now was their moment for taking control.

So half of them suddenly stood in a row,
like dancers in some sort of musical show.
They spread out their tentacles, weaving them all
with the others beside them, creating a wall.

Then they came forward, inch after inch,
enclosing their prey in a sinister pinch.
So Morty and Winnie and all of the rest,
were hemmed in a corner, compacted, compressed.

They were forced in a clumsy, uncomfortable pose,
being elbow to elbow to shoulder to nose;
and being so crowded, so awkwardly crammed,
they couldn't fight back. They were thoroughly jammed!

Then the Octomabots, who were still in the air,
could pluck up their prey without even a care.
In this way, the creatures were quickly re-caught,
in spite of how bravely their battle was fought.

The Behemoth, at last, was the only one left;
but even with all his incredible heft,
he couldn't fight back; his chances were slim.
There were simply too many—even for him!

So alas, my good reader, the battle was done,
and the Octomabots had clumsily won.

The creatures of Earth, I'm sorry to say,
were locked up again, without any delay.
The bolts were refastened, the cages refilled,
and Morty, of course, wasn't terribly thrilled.

Once more, he was hunched on the floor of his cell,
and wondering: *Where was Katrina Katrell?!*

Understandably, Morty was all in a huff.
"Adventures!" he grumbled. "Enough is enough!"

Then the entranceway door, it opened up wide,
and Dullbert came wearily strolling inside.
He stood for a moment, one hand on his hip,
the other one thoughtfully tapping his lip.

He took a step forward and finally spoke.
"So, you tried to escape? Oh, please! What a joke.
There's no way to leave here, or didn't you know?
We're up on the moon! There's nowhere to *go!*"
He's right, Morty thought, feeling thoroughly beat,
beset by a feeling of utter defeat.

He puffed out a rather disheartening sigh.
While Winnie (as usual) started to cry.
But just as she started to sob in her cell,
her tears were cut short by the toll of a bell.

It resounded like thunder. It rang and it rang.
It chimed with a terrible, desperate *clang!!*
Hearing it, Dullbert was suddenly tense.
"The alarms?" he exclaimed. "That doesn't make sense!"

He examined his cages, dismayed and distraught.
There's one of them missing! he suddenly thought.

To Morty he said, "Hey you, with the fur.
That girl who you came with, what happened to her?"
He went to his bank of surveillance displays,
showing dungeons and cells in an intricate maze.
He let out a shriek as he peered at the screen:

"HOLY GADZ*OOK*AHS!
Not inside the machine!"

He stabbed at some buttons (he pushed quite a few),
and the Hoarder of Boredom split open in two,
revealing Katrina, who cowered inside.
She had nowhere to go. She had nowhere to hide.
But amid all those wires and Graylian gear,
all that anyone saw was the luminous sphere.

You see, my good reader, that circle of glass,
was filling with billows of *colorful* gas!

Where once it was filled with a nebulous gray,
the Tedium Steam was all washing away.
It was being replaced with the colorful threads,
of a gas made of glittering yellows and reds;
and not only those, but a great many more,
more colors than anyone's thought of before!

There was olive and orange and lavender, too!
There was purple and puce and cerulean blue!
There was violet, vermillion, viridian-green!
More colors, I'd say, than you've ever seen!

They were blindingly bright, seeming never to cease:
There was burgundy, lilac, and even cerise,
all mingling with others (like aquamarine),
swirling and whirling inside the machine!

Dullbert just stood there in shock and dismay,
He was utterly stunned, didn't know what to say.
He whimpered and waggled his Graylian head.
"You didn't!" he cried. *"You couldn't!"* he said.

"You're wrong," said Katrina, "I certainly could.
I fixed it all up...I fixed it up good!"

"Fixed it?! You *wrecked* it! How incredibly mean!
You've demolished my Hoarder of Boredom Machine!"
"Not at all," said Katrina, shaking her head.
"It's not wrecked. It's not broken. It's *better* instead!"

"You rascal!" cried Dullbert. "You're lying to me!"
He lowered his voice, in a pitiful plea.
"Listen, Katrina," he said with a sigh,
"without boredom for fuel, my planet…will die."

"Wait," said Katrina, "see, this is my hunch:
This *new* kind of gas packs a powerful punch."
Dullbert was doubtful. He wasn't convinced.
He gaped at the colors. He grimaced and winced.
"Katrina, just look at it—*puff* after *puff*…
It's disgusting! What is it, this *colorful* stuff?!"

Katrina just smiled, and turning around,
she admired the wonderful substance she found.

She folded her arms, looking up at the glass.
"I think that I'll call it:

Enchantium *Gas!"*

En

CHAPTER 18
Enchantium *what?!*

Enchantium what?!”

was Dullbert’s reply.
“I imagine you think I’m a gullible guy!
‘Enchantium Gas?’ It’s a fib! It’s a hoax!
It’s a trick, as they say, with mirrors and smokes!”

"But no," said Katrina, "I'm willing to bet
this stuff has more power than anything yet!"

"Colors?!" cried Dullbert. "They're useless! They're junk!
And to claim they have *power?* That's nothing but bunk!"
He turned to the dials and his video screen.
"Just look at these gauges, you'll see what I mean."

But guess what, my good reader. Katrina was right!
To Dullbert's surprise (and to Dullbert's delight),
his energy gauges were spinning like mad,
much faster, you see, than they formerly had.

"Amazing!" breathed Dullbert. "In fact, you're correct!
There's more energy here than I'd ever expect!
But Katrina," he whispered, "what did you do?
This substance—it's almost too good to be true!"

But of course it was true, and Katrina explained
her modification was simply attained
by giving the wires a bit of a snip,
switching them round in a bit of a flip.

In reversing the flow, she had hoped to coerce
the whole apparatus to work in reverse.
In place of a steam that was dreary and dim,
it sought out a gas full of vigor and vim!

(And if you don't believe such a vapor exists,
a gas made of vibrantly colorful mists,
then shut your eyes now, scrunch them up tight!
And you'll see it—like flashes of colourful light.

That's how it begins, as thoughts in your mind.
They spiral and tumble, they whirl and unwind.
Like Tedium Steam, they come out of your head—
but not when you're bored,
        when you're *thinking* instead.)

"I'm sorry," said Dullbert, "for being so cruel.
This '*Enchantium Gas*' is a far better fuel.

You've convinced me, Katrina. I have to concede:
I see now *enchantment's* the thing that we need.
Excitement and wonder, amusement and mirth—
That's what we need from the people of Earth!"

Then he turned to his panel of buttons and light.
"Okay then," he said, "let's put everything right."
He led everyone out of their cages and crates,
and down to the somber Moonagerie gates.

There, rising up like the pipes on a stove,
like a thicket of trees in a curious grove,
were the Graylian rockets, preparing for flight,
rumbling and steaming and teeming with light.

"Here we are," Dullbert said, with a generous grin.
"All aboard everyone! Let's get everyone in!"

The first to climb up was Katrina Katrell,
then all of the creatures (the zorgles as well),
until all were aboard, the great and the small,
with the lonely Behemoth the last of them all.

Then the rockets took off! They went spiraling high,
through the glitter of stars and the black of the sky. . .

Meanwhile, on Earth, very little had changed.
Papers were shuffled and goods were exchanged.
Most people, you see, were the same as before.
They were leading their lives, no less and no more,

stuck in their offices, buildings and cars,
never once looking up at the twinkle of stars.

(To so many people, the world was a bore.
It might even remind you of Graybalon-Four...)

So perhaps you'd imagine their utter surprise
when early one evening, from out of the skies,
came an army of Graylian rockets from space,
sweeping out of the clouds at a perilous pace.

They arrived and alighted with effortless ease,
like feathers at play on a delicate breeze.
When the dust settled down, the doors opened wide,
and creatures came out of the cabins inside.
The crowds that had gathered all pointed in fear.
Nearly everyone thought that *invaders* were here.

They shrieked when the steps of the rockets unfurled,
"Monsters!" they cried. "They're invading the world!"

But then they saw something they didn't expect.
It extinguished their panic. It made them reflect.
What they saw was a girl, just a regular child.
She waved to them all. She nodded and smiled.

At her side was a creature, all covered with hair.
A warthog, perhaps...or maybe a bear.
Well, whatever it was, it was certainly weird.
It had horns on its head and a whiskery beard.

The TV reporters, they clustered and swarmed.
"What happened?!" they cried. "We must be informed!"

The girl was accosted with cameras and mics.
They were waved in her face like skewers and spikes.

The reporters cried, *"Who?!"* The reporters cried, *"How?!"*
"What, when and where?! You must tell us, right now!"

The girl found her voice. It was clear as a bell.
"My name," she explained, "is

Katrina Katrell

These creatures aren't *aliens*, isn't that clear?
They don't come from space.
They come from right here."

Everyone gaped, they ogled and glared.
They gawked, rather rudely, and everyone stared.
That's when they knew, with the merest of looks,
that these were the creatures from stories and books!

So they yelped with a joy they could barely conceal.
The creatures weren't myths! They were *actually real!*
In that very moment, the people were changed.
Their minds were expanded, their thoughts rearranged.

Enchantment was coursing through all of their veins.
It swept through their bodies and into their brains,

where a pressure built up, like a teakettle pot,
It grew and it grew, then it popped like a shot!

It flew out all at once! It spiraled and swirled!
It *erupted* from people all over the world!
For the very first time in a great many years,
Enchantium Gases came out of their ears!

Then everyone watched as the creatures dispersed.
It began with the merfolk, they were the first.
They wished to return to the fish and the foam,
and the wind and the waves of their watery home.

The phoenixes then set their bodies ablaze,
and took to the sky like a flock of *flambés*.
Then went the pixies, the ogres, the gnomes,
who trundled away to their forested homes.
The yetis were next. They went lumbering off,
each one of them fluffing their flocculent coif.

The griffins and gargoyles said their goodbyes,
and leapt from their feet and into the skies.

The sphinxes, gorgons, the Gillygaloo,
the satyrs, the centaurs, the hippogriff too—
they all headed home, after bidding farewell
to their savior…a girl named Katrina Katrell.

At last, the Behemoth went *thrumping* away
(but where he was going—well, no one could say).

Then bidding goodbye to the windigo clans,
Katrina shook each of their leathery hands.
Winnie stepped up, and Katrina was squeezed
so breathlessly tight that she started to wheeze.

Next was the zorgle named Cyril DeYoung.
(the finest of flingers who ever had flung).
"Kiddo," he said, in his leisurely drawl,
"I bet you'd be deadly at Zorgally Ball."
Then he and the zorgles, the windigo too,
went back to the mountains of Zorgamazoo.

Dullbert came forward to bid his goodbye.
"Katrina," he said, "I promise to try

to rescue my race from its Graylian haze.
The time has arrived for changing our ways.
I'll give them a bit of enlightened advice:
that sometimes, a *little* excitement is nice.
That's what I'll do—start spreading the word!
Or my name's not Dullbert Hohummer, the Third!"

Then to Katrina's tremendous surprise
the tiniest sparkle came into his eyes,
and a smidgeon of color came into his face,
as he climbed in his rocket…and flew into space.

Once Dullbert was gone, once the rockets had flown,
Katrina and Morty were standing alone.

Katrina said, "Well…" as she nodded her head.
"Our adventure is finished. It's over," she said.
She regarded her friend with a wavering smile.
She put out her hand. It hung there a while.

Morty reached out and he gave it a tug,
and their handshake, abruptly, turned into a hug.
Then Morty stepped back. He mumbled and frowned.
He explained it was time to go back underground.

He'd had more than his fill of adventuring stuff.
It was time to go home, back to Underwood Bluff.
He was long overdue at the Hospital Shop.
He had to return and check on his Pop.

With the gleam of a tear in each of their eyes,
Katrina and Mortimer said their goodbyes.
Then Morty turned round, moving terribly slow,
as Katrina stood wistfully watching him go.

His shoulders were slackened. He shuffled his feet,
approaching the steps that went under the street.
He followed them down, going lower, and then:
he vanished. He was back in the shadows again.

By now, my good reader, the crowd had so thinned,
the only things left were the whispers of wind.
And Katrina recalled, in a moment of woe:
that she, of all others, had nowhere to go.

It was just as she pondered this worrying fact,
that somewhere nearby, something *rattled* and *clacked*.
A sound like a dustbin of rubbish and soot,
being clumsily kicked by a ham-fisted foot.

"Hello, my dear,"

said a voice from the past.

"I've finally found you! We're together at last!"

The voice had a screechy, contemptible tone,
and Katrina could tell:

It was Mrs. Krabone!

She came out of the dark, where she'd carefully hid.
"I missed you," she said. "I mean, really I did."

Her expression was odd. It was haggard and bleak.
She was unlike herself. She looked humble and meek.

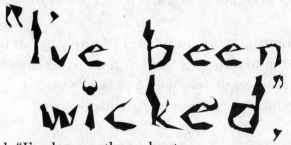

"I've been wicked,"

she said. "I've been rather a brute.
I've been spiteful and vile, and a villain to boot.
But seeing those creatures, those beasties and things,
they tugged at my heart—at its innermost strings!

Those magical creatures untangled my knots.
I was lit from within! And with thousands of watts!
It changed me for good. It made me think twice.
No more nasty, I thought. Instead…I'll be nice."

She spread out her arms. She opened them wide.
She smiled and invited Katrina inside.

Katrina, of course, didn't know what to do.

She hoped that the words she was hearing were true.
She wished that Old Krabby had honestly changed,
and was no longer hateful or cruel or deranged.

What Katrina most craved, as I'm sure you can tell,
was someone who loved her and treated her well.
She wanted some semblance of family ties,
upon which a childhood so greatly relies.

So she took a step forward, with hope in her heart:

This moment,

perhaps,
would be

A

NEW

START...

CHAPTER 19
say *goodbye* to your brain

atrina,

however, had made a mistake.

Old Krabby's compunction was utterly fake.
"Gotcha!" she cried, with a snatch and a grab,
with a pinch and pull, like the claw of a crab.
Things only got worse, I'm afraid to report,

when out of the murk, came a snickering snort.
It was followed by figures, and each of them foul.
They surrounded Katrina, like wolves on the prowl.

"Katrina, hello there," said Doctor LeFang.
"Look who we met. Such a nice little gang!"

Katrina looked left. Katrina looked right.
Both sides held an equally worrying sight.
There was the ruffian, SICKLY VAN PUKE,
his nose spilling over with gobbledygook.

Selena the Slash was waiting as well,
to exact her revenge on Katrina Katrell.
And those two, of course, were never without:
BUGSY MCCROOK, that unbearable lout!

He was wearing a typically simpering leer.
He took a step forward and said, with a sneer,

"Your weird little pals—they ain't here anymore.
So I'd say it's time that we settled the score!"
In seconds, the villains were closing the gap.
It was clear she'd been caught in a terrible trap!

Selena and SICKLY snuck up from the rear.
They captured Katrina by elbow and ear.
They twisted her arms, holding her tight,
while Dr. LeFang stood off to the right.

In his hand were the blades of his wicked device,
especially made to puncture and slice.
In the lamplight it flashed with a sinister gleam,
like the teeth of a beast in a hideous dream.

He raised up his Mincer, holding it high.
"I shall enter," he said, "just here, by your eye.
So don't move a muscle, or you may feel some pain,
because now, my dear girl,

say
goodbye
to your
brain!"

"Stop!"

came a voice. It came from the street.
It seemed to rise up from under their feet.

A manhole popped open and clambering out,
came Morty himself, like a flowering sprout.
"Hey, grimwits," he said. "Whatever you planned,
you'd better just quit it, do you understand?"

This time, however, the gang was prepared.
BUGSY was grinning. He didn't look scared.

"So it's you again, is it?" he said with a sneer.
"Well, listen, I'll make myself perfectly clear:
You frightened us once, way back in our den,
but trust me, you freak, you won't do it again!"

BUGSY stepped forward, the head of the gang,
and so did that lunatic, Doctor LeFang.

He was staring at Morty (or rather his head).
"What a curious beast!" he excitedly said.
"How I would certainly love to obtain
such a wholly unique and unusual brain!"

"Well, sorry," said Morty, "to mess with your plot,
but I'm *using* my brain, believe it or not.
And **BUGSY**, you're no longer frightened of me?
Well, how 'bout my friend? He's as big as a tree."

All of a sudden, everything shook
(including the nerves of **BUGSY MCCROOK**).
The buildings, the cars, and even the street,
went *tharumpah-tharump* to a walloping beat.

The **Behemoth**, of course,
that voluminous chap,
whose footfalls were each like a thundering clap,
stepped into the alley, his hands on his hips.
He was looking half-starved. He was licking his lips.

"I'm famished!" he boomed, surveying the scene.
"And I *love* eating folks who're nasty and mean.

Their blood is so salty! Their livers so firm!
Whenever you eat them, they wriggle and squirm!

Their skin has a scent like the stinkiest cheese!
And their heads—
they go *pop* like the plumpest of peas!
You can bake them in pastry to make a soufflé,
or perhaps for dessert, a meanie parfait!
Whichever the case, I chew them to pulp!
I guzzle them down, with a slurp and a gulp!"

"Well, then," said Morty, a smile on his face.
"Let me tell you, my friend—*you're in just the right place.*"

BUGSY MCCROOK, and the rest of his gang,
and Mrs. Krabone and Doctor LeFang,
they didn't stand gaping for even a flash.
Instead, they ran off in a blundering dash.

The Behemoth, meanwhile, that insatiable brute,
he chased them away in *tharumping* pursuit.
"Come back here," he cried, "You sumptuous bums!
At least let me nibble your fingers and thumbs!"

But they didn't come back. They were brisk!
    They were brusque!
They went scampering off in the darkening dusk,
weeping like babies and shaking like leaves,
wiping their snot on the ends of their sleeves.

As they ran, all you heard were their pitiful moans,
for the fear in their hearts had spread into their bones.
Their running was clumsy, with twitches and hops,
as they stumbled and bumbled in blundering flops,
wailing and whining and yelping and then:

They were gone.

They weren't ever heard from again.

Turning to Morty, Katrina said, "*Hey!*
You know something, Mort? You just saved the day!
That's pretty heroic. It's terribly brave.
What a very *adventurous* way to behave!"

"Aw, shucks," Morty said. "Well, maybe you're right.
You could say I put up a pretty good fight!
Or maybe not *me*," he said with a smirk.
"I suppose the Behemoth did most of the work.
Besides, if whatever you're saying is true,
any courage I showed—I learned it from you."

Katrina was flattered, but she didn't agree.
"No, Morty," she said, "it wasn't from me.
If we're speaking of courage, you got it all wrong.
You're just like your Pop. It was there all along."

No words could make Morty feel better than those.
He was pleased, from his horns to the tips of his toes.
Katrina, however, felt sullen and low,
recalling, again, she had nowhere to go.

She looked up at Morty, and then looked away.
In her heart, she wanted to ask him to stay.

But instead she looked down, her chin on her chest.
It's over, she thought. *It's the end of our quest.*
She looked up again and thought, with a smile:
But maybe I'll visit him, once in a while.

"Now wait," Morty said, "There's no need to be glum.
You ought to remember:

I'm always your chum!"

Then he chuckled a bit. "I should really have known
you'd end up in a jam if I left you alone.
So listen, Katrina, come live underground,
under the streets, where us zorgles are found."

Katrina was pleased. She nodded her head.
"I'd like that," she whispered. It was all that she said.

"Well, great!" Morty beamed. "In that case, let's go!
Let me show you my home in the tunnels below!
I can see it already! You and me and my Pop!
That's the first place we'll go—to the Hospital Shop!
So we better get moving, it's already late,
because visiting hours are over at eight!"

CHAPTER 20

the rest of their *days*

Bortlebee Yorgle lay under the street.
Or more to the point,
he lay under a sheet,

tucked in like a child, from his chin to his heels,
in a bed that could travel on four little wheels.

So yes, he was cozy, but sick to his bones;
his words, when he spoke, were like pitiful groans.
His pallor was pale, he was barely alive.
His doctors were certain he wouldn't survive.

But when he saw Morty step into his room,
the pink of his cheeks came back into bloom.

"Pop!" Morty gushed, and ran to his side.
"This adventure we had was one heck of a ride!"
He started recounting the tale to his Pop,
who silently gestured for Morty to stop.

"I already know," said his Pop, with a laugh.
"I heard the good news on my radiograph:
You bravely set off and when you were through,
you'd rescued the zorgles of Zorgamazoo!"

"Well, yes," Morty said, "the zorgles and more!
There were all sorts of creatures from legend and lore.
There were *thousands* of others we rescued, as well,
all thanks to Katrina—Katrina Katrell."

And so she came in. She stood by the wall.
All along, she'd been waiting, just out in the hall.
She came forward, approaching old Bortlebee's bed.
"It's an honor to finally meet you," she said.

Bortlebee groaned. He shifted his weight.
He coughed and his throat seemed to rumble and grate;
his lungs made a noise like a wheeze or a whine.
"The honor," he sputtered, "is entirely mine."

Katrina was blushing. She looked at her feet,
and soon, she was nearly as red as a beet.
"Please, sir," she said, "I hope you can see
that Morty's as much of a hero as me.

He saved me not once, but actually twice.
He's given me constant support and advice.
He's taught me that sometimes you'll land in a jam,
when you're hasty and brash…in the way that I am;
and I think that I've learned that life can be rough
if you're *overly* drawn to adventuring stuff.

But that's what I love: An adventurous quest!
In some ways, I know—I'm sort of obsessed.

Not Morty, mind you. He hates having 'thrills.'
If he'd had a choice, he'd have run for the hills.
But that's not what he did. No, Mortimer *stayed,*
in spite of the fact he was clearly afraid.
In that way, I think, he's different from me.
In that way…he's braver than I'll ever be.
I guess what I mean is, I think you could say,
that *Morty's* the number-one hero today."

Bortlebee smiled. "He's a hero. It's true.
It's something, you see, that I already knew."
Wincing with pain, he looked up at his son.
"In my eyes," he whispered, "he's second to none."

Bortlebee beckoned, with a quavering hand.
"Now, both of you listen. You must understand:
Soon I'll be gone. I'll cash in my chips.
My very last breath will pass over my lips.

And son, after that, you'll be all alone.
You'll be just like Katrina: You'll be on your own.
Adventures, however, turn strangers to kin,

and kin stick together, in thickness and thin.
So I want you to promise, I want you to *vow*,
you'll look after each other. You're like family now."

Katrina leaned forward. She nodded her head.
"We know what you mean. And we promise," she said.

"Pop?" Morty asked. "Hey, Pop, you okay?"
But his Pop didn't move, in the bed where he lay.

Had it happened? thought Morty. *Had it finally come?*
Just to think it made Morty feel utterly numb.

But then Bortlebee smiled—just the tiniest grin,
a smile that belied a great glowing within.
"I'm proud of you, son," he happily sighed.
And then Bortlebee Yorgle…he quietly died.

Don't worry, my reader.
No need to be sad.

A death isn't always entirely bad.
Among zorgles, for instance, a life that is long,
is a life best remembered with dancing and song.

Any Zorgledom funeral bubbles with fun—
when the life-before-death was a jovial one;
and since Bortlebee died so delightfully old,
his interment was hardly unhappy or cold.
Instead, it was bursting with music and mirth,
celebrating his *life*, from the day of his birth!

His casket was spangled in ribbons and flags
and streamers emblazoned with ziggles and zags.
They flapped as his coffin was carried away,
up to Zorgamazoo, on the following day.

The guests in attendance had gathered around
a great swelling of earth: the burial mound.
And oh, what a crowd! One thousand, or more,
and not only zorgles, but creatures galore!
When they heard it was Bortlebee Yorgle who died,
they came from all corners, from far and from wide!

The yetis arrived with the dragons and elves;
and the ogres, of course, who came by themselves.
There were flubbery creatures from various lochs
and phoenixes, flaming in flurrying flocks.

Winnie, as well—she came with her clans,
from the cliffs that encompassed the windigo lands.
There was even the magical Gillygaloo,
and, of course, every zorgle from Zorgamazoo!

Every creature he'd met, every singular beast,
they all had arrived, for the funeral-feast!

Although Morty was saddened and stricken with grief,
his feelings of sorrow were thankfully brief.
When he saw all the people his father had known,
he realized at once that he wasn't alone.
They were all the same creatures—he'd met them as well,
in the course of his quest with Katrina Katrell!

These here were his friends—they had come by the ton!
They'd been passed, so it seemed, from father to son.

So wiping a tear from the edge of his eye,
Morty rose from his seat. He straightened his tie.
He then began singing the eulogy song,
with everyone dancing, and singing along…

Later, when the evening had come to a close,
the guests all departed for rest and repose.
Having paid their respects, they gently withdrew
to the huts and cabins of Zorgamazoo.

In one little cottage, just out of the way,
made of thatches of bramble and timber and clay,

and built in a tree that was ample and wide,
a trio of friends were relaxing inside.

In one chair, a zorgle, curled up in his coat,
a weatherworn necktie adorning his throat.
The second, a creature all hairy with curls
that were pale like the shimmer of elegant pearls.
The third of the trio, the oddest of all,
wasn't hairy or scary, and not very tall;
just a regular girl, no less and no more,
but the sort of a girl whom you couldn't ignore,
a girl you would think was imagining things,
like pirates and gadgets and creatures and kings!

They each had a cushion, a comfortable seat.
They were having some cocoa and something to eat.
They were curled by the fire, with blankets as well:
Winnie and Morty…and Katrina Katrell.

So now, as we come to the end of my text, I'll tell you a little of what happened next.

Winnie returned to her family clans,
to the bats, and the balls, and the roar of the fans.
After all, her first love, as I'm sure you recall,
is that wonderful game they call Zorgally Ball.

She went back to the fields where she usually played,
to stadiums dappled with sun and with shade,
to the places where often she walloped and swung,
in the bush-leagues—with Cyril Zipzorgle DeYoung.

Morty, meanwhile, he also went back;
he returned to his job as a newspaper hack.
Rejoining the crew at the *Rumor Review*,
he typed up the saga of Zorgamazoo.

Each week, a new chapter would go to the press,
and the story became a resounding success!
People who read it were rather amazed
(in addition, the telling was critically praised).

And no matter who read it, from toddler and tyke
to queasy old geezers and wheezers alike—
any reader at all, in spite of their years,

had *Enchantium Gas* coming out of their ears!
For with all zorgle stories, for better or worse,
the whole of the telling was written in verse.

Some called it madness. Others called it sublime,
for he penned the whole story *completely in rhyme!*
And the tale, my good reader, you must understand
is the same one you're holding, right now, in your hand.

And what of Katrina,
Katrina Katrell?
That story, perhaps, is too lengthy to tell.
She traveled the world on *adventures* galore;
she went roaming all over, had so many more!

On all of them, Morty was there at her side
(it seemed he was always along for the ride),
on travels and treks that would always amaze;
the two would be friends for the rest of their days...

Days that were spent in a world of surprise,
a world in which phoenixes lit up the skies,

a world of more wonder than ever before,
where pixies were back in the cracks in the floor,
where serpents and mermaids were back in the seas,
and ogres went loping though forests and trees.

A world where mysterious creatures were found,
in tunnels meandering under the ground!
Or on mountains above us! Or deep in the grass!

A world all awhirl with

Enchantium Gas!

That's it, my good reader.

My story is done.
And my, what a strange and mysterious one!
But that was the story I wanted to tell:
The story of me and Katrina Katrell.

And so, my good reader,
or perhaps my good friend,
we have come to the finish,

the curtain,

The

End.

ACKNOWLEDGMENTS

A novel in rhyme is a risky experiment. To some, it's OUTRIGHT MADNESS. So I wish to thank my family and friends for their unremitting faith in my lunacy. In particular, I wish express gratitude to the following people for their kind and thoughtful assistance with the various aspects of the book: Linda Svenson, Keith Maillard, Meryn Cadell, and most of all, Alison Acheson, at the University of British Columbia; Jessica Rothenberg, Ben Schrank and the enthusiastic team at Razorbill Books; Jackie Kaiser and the wonderful people at Westwood Creative Artists; Laura Dodwell-Groves, Christy Goerzen, Maryn Brown, Adam Higgs and everyone else from 2005's CRWR-503; Victor Rivas for his enchanting artwork; Natalie Sousa, Christian Fuenfhausen, Benjamin Wood, Nick Wood and the members of "the THC" (Terry Dove, Carla Gillis, Sarah Leavitt, Susan Olding and Joe Wiebe); and the talented engineers at Ignition Recording Studios in London.

Finally, my eternal gratitude to Hana, without whom, this book would not exist; your love and support is unwavering and miraculous.